DOCTOR WHO
FOUR TO DOOMSDAY

D1159479

DOCTOR WHO
FOUR TO DOOMSDAY

Based on the BBC television serial by Terence Dudley by arrangement with the British Broadcasting Corporation

Terrance Dicks

No. 77
in the
Doctor Who Library

A TARGET BOOK

published by
the Paperback Division of
W. H. ALLEN & Co. Ltd

A Target Book
Published in 1983
By the Paperback Division of
W.H. Allen & Co. Ltd
A Howard & Wyndham Company
44 Hill Street, London W1X 8LB

First published in Great Britain by
W.H. Allen & Co. Ltd 1983

Printed and bound in Great Britain by
Hunt Barnard Printing Ltd, Aylesbury, Bucks.

ISBN 0 426 19334 2

CONTENTS

1

Ship of Mystery

The ship was like a city. The complex multi-hulled shape slid silently through the blackness of space, powerful, sinister, determined.

The ship's journey was nearly over. It was four days away from Earth.

The interior was as impressive as the exterior: enormous high-ceilinged chambers, elaborately decorated walls of gleaming metal; long, echoing corridors and walkways, lifts and stairways and ramps leading between different levels.

Something very strange was about to happen on this ship.

The vaulted chamber was vast, silent and deserted. It was filled with incredibly sophisticated scientific equipment, great towers and columns and mazes of it, lights flashing in transparent neon-lit spirals, instrument panels lining the walls, free-standing consoles dotted here and there, a bewildering vista of elaborate instrumentation, stretching away into the distance. The place was silent and deserted.

A strange wheezing and groaning sound broke the cathedral-like hush.

A square blue shape materialised out of nowhere, and suddenly a rather battered old police box was standing against one gleaming metal wall. It looked *very* out of place.

Inside the box, however, was a technology even more advanced than that which surrounded it, because this particular police box wasn't a police box at all. It was a TARDIS—an acronym of the words Time And Relative Dimensions in Space. The TARDIS was dimensionally transcendental.

Inside was an impossibly large control room, dominated by a many-sided central control console. In the centre of the console was a transparent column called the time rotor. When the TARDIS was in flight, the column rose and fell steadily. At the moment, it was slowly coming to a stop.

Two young people were watching the process in thoughtful silence. The first was an attractive-looking girl with brown hair and an aristocratic, somewhat haughty air. She wore a kind of velvet trouser-suit with elaborately puffed sleeves. Her name was Nyssa, and she came originally from a planet called Traken.

Beside her was a smallish, round-faced youth wearing a yellow tunic. At the moment he was looking rather solemn, though his normal expression was one of cheerful impudence. His name was Adric.

Both Adric and Nyssa had joined the Doctor in a series of dangerous adventures. Both were now reconciled to the fact that they were unlikely to see their home worlds again. Nyssa had left Traken after the tragic death of her father, and since Adric's home planet, Alzarius, was in another universe, there was little chance of his getting back there even if he wanted to, which he didn't as it happened. Adric had been a bit of a rebel on his home planet. He still was, even in the TARDIS.

The column juddered to a halt.

'Well, we've stopped,' said Adric unnecessarily. 'We're here! Get the Doctor, Nyssa, will you?'

Nyssa wondered if Adric's tendency to bossiness came from the fact that he'd been travelling in the TARDIS longer than she had, or if it was just because he was male and she was female. Probably he just had a bossy nature anyway. Still, this was no time for a quarrel, not now they were just about to lose one of their companions.

'All right,' said Nyssa. As she turned to leave the control room, two more people came in.

The first was the Doctor himself. He was now in his fifth incarnation, and seemed to be growing younger rather than older. In his present form he was a rather slight, fair-haired young man with a pleasant, open face. He wore the dress of an Edwardian cricketer—striped trousers, fawn coat with red piping, a white cricketing sweater and an open-necked shirt. The whole ensemble was completed for reasons best known to himself by a sprig of celery in the lapel.

Close behind the Doctor came his third, least willing companion, an Australian air hostess called Tegan Jovanka. Tegan had become involved with the Doctor just before his fifth regeneration when she had entered the TARDIS in the mistaken belief that it was a real

9

police box. Since then she had been carried through a series of bewildering and terrifying adventures, demanding stridently all the time to be taken back to Earth. As far as Tegan was concerned, she had been hijacked and she wanted things put right as soon as possible.

Members of twentieth-century Australian culture are not noted for shyness or reticence. Tegan could be exceptionally forceful, even for an Australian. When she wanted something done she made sure that everybody knew it.

The Doctor had made several attempts to get her back home again, but thanks to a certain erratic quality in the TARDIS's steering mechanisms, none of them had quite worked out.

'We've arrived, Doctor,' said Adric again.

The Doctor nodded. 'A bit ahead of time, I think. What was your flight, Tegan?'

'Flight AA778, 1730 hours.'

The Doctor studied the temporal indicator panel. 'February 28th, 1981, and it's only 1615 hours. You'll have time for a cup of tea!'

Adric touched a control, and the TARDIS scanner screen slid into view, revealing a vista of strangely shaped instruments and flashing lights.

Tegan looked doubtfully at it. 'Doesn't look very much like London Airport to me.'

The Doctor moved to her side. 'Last time I was here they were doing extraordinary things to Terminal Three—' He broke off. 'No, you're right, it doesn't.'

Adric said indignantly, 'Don't look at me! I set the co-ordinates precisely as you instructed. Six, three zero

10

and niner, zero – in the inner spiral arm of Galaxia Kyklos.'

Tegan stared at him. 'Look, I want Heathrow, on the M4—not Corfu.'

'Adric's showing off,' said the Doctor gently. 'He means the Milky Way. *Your* galaxy, Tegan.' He studied the TARDIS's instruments. 'There seems to have been a massive magnetic-field shift as well ...'

Adric was staring at the screen. 'Looks like a control room to me.'

'I suppose it could be part of the Piccadilly Line,' said the Doctor hopefully.

Tegan said acidly, 'Oh great! I can go the rest of the way by train.'

The Doctor checked map-readings. 'I'll tell you something else. The atmosphere's all wrong.'

'What's wrong with it?'

'A diminution of oxygen and nitrogen, and traces of a mercurial compound. *And* there's intense proton activity ...' Muttering to himself, the Doctor disappeared through the door that led to the interior of the TARDIS.

Nyssa said, 'I thought Earth was relatively primitive at this period?'

'Oh, did you?' said Tegan indignantly.

'That instrumentation out there seems very advanced.' Nyssa pointed to a complex installation assembled on one of the free-standing consoles. 'That looks like a resonant stroboscope.'

'And what's that when it's at home?' demanded Tegan.

Nyssa gave her a puzzled look. 'But it is at home.'

The Doctor returned carrying a gleaming metal helmet with a transparent visor and a complex miniaturised life-support system built into the back. 'I'm going outside to take a look. None of you is to leave here, is that clearly understood?'

Three mutinous faces glared back at him.

'Good,' said the Doctor cheerfully. The outer doors slid open and the Doctor went outside.

'Well!' said Tegan. For once she was lost for words.

The Doctor stood staring interestedly at the maze of equipment all around him. It was rather like being inside a giant pin-table machine, he thought. 'Control room? Or laboratory? I wonder ...'

He spotted a porthole and moved over to it. Outside he saw the blackness of deep space, sprinkled with the myriad stars of the Milky Way. They were in the right place, at any rate.

Fascinated, baffled, and more than a little apprehensive, the Doctor continued his tour. Since he didn't look upwards, he failed to notice the gleaming metal globe with its single unblinking eye that hovered just a few feet above his head.

In a different part of the ship, three pairs of eyes were focused on a bank of monitor screens, one of which showed the Doctor as he prowled about the control room.

'I would see the intrusion again.' The voice was deep, commanding, with a throaty, almost croaking quality.

The TARDIS appeared on the monitor screen.

'Well?' said the deep voice.

A female voice said, 'It is not in my memory.'

A third voice, masculine like the first, but younger, clearer, said, 'Nor in mine.'

The commanding voice said, 'I would look again at the humanoid.'

The Doctor appeared on the screen.

Tegan sighed. 'He's taking his time.'

Adric nodded. 'Yes. I've never known him hurry anything.'

'Is there another of those helmet things?'

'The space-packs? Plenty of them.'

'He told us to stay here,' said Nyssa firmly.

Tegan looked at the screen. 'What's he doing? Perhaps he's in trouble.'

'He's always in trouble,' said Adric. 'Haven't you noticed? It amuses him.'

'Well, it doesn't amuse me. He promised to get me on my flight. He'll lose me my job.'

'Oh no, he won't. Be patient.'

'Patient?' screamed Tegan. 'After all I've been through since I came through that door. Not to mention my poor aunt reduced to *that* long.' Dramatically Tegan held out her hands, like an angler describing a very small fish. 'Patient! You must be joking.'

'Listen,' said Adric wearily. 'We're fifth-dimensional in this thing. We have the facility of time-travel. He can still get you on your flight, even if he's out there a week.'

'And what do we do in the meantime?'

'You could always read.'

'*Read*?' Tegan spoke as if reading was some totally

13

outrageous and unheard-of activity.

'Yes. There's a fascinating book on mathematics back there by a man called Bert Russell.'

'Maths!' said Tegan scornfully.

'That's the trouble with women,' muttered Adric. 'Mindless, impatient and bossy.'

Tegan glared accusingly at him. 'I heard that— chauvinist!'

'You were meant to hear it.'

'I heard it too,' said Nyssa calmly. She held up a massive copy of *Principia Mathematica* by Bertrand Russell. 'Is this the book you meant?' Nyssa had picked up the book and skimmed quickly through it. She'd found it quite interesting in an elementary sort of way. 'Mindless, am I?'

Adric looked a little shamefaced. 'Yes, well. You're not a woman, are you?'

'I'm not?'

'No, you're only a girl.' Satisfied that he'd had the last word, Adric went back to his calculations.

The three pairs of eyes were still observing the Doctor on the monitor screens. He was still pottering about amongst the banks of equipment. As they watched the intruder looked up and grinned cheerfully at the three watchers.

The deep, throaty voice said, 'He knows that he is observed.'

The lighter, female voice said, 'What an enchanting smile!'

Nyssa looked at the scanner screen for the hundredth

14

time. 'Still no sign of him.'

Adric shrugged. 'Can't be far.'

'How do you know?'

Adric was studying the readings on the console. 'By the look of things we're on some kind of spaceship. There's a limit to how far he *can* go. He must be on board somewhere.'

'You can't be sure of that. Even if we are on some kind of spacecraft, it could be enormous.' Nyssa studied the view on the scanner screen and pointed to another piece of equipment, just visible on the edge of the screen. 'Just look at that!'

Adric looked. 'So? What does it do?'

'It increases density.'

'What for?'

'To reduce matter, of course.'

'What matter?'

'The Doctor's, perhaps?'

'That's ridiculous.'

'Is it?' Nyssa glanced at Tegan and then looked away. Matter-compression was a particularly agonising form of death. It was a favourite method of the Master. It was the way he'd destroyed Tegan's aunt.

Adric looked at Nyssa, then back at the screen. Nyssa was just being alarmist, he thought. Irrational, fanciful—in a word, female. But then—the Doctor had been gone for a very long time . . .

2

A Meeting with Monarch

By now the Doctor was well aware of the metal globe floating over his head, following him silently wherever he went. He studied it thoughtfully. It seemed to study him back. The Doctor gave it a cheery smile and made his way back to the TARDIS.

Three pairs of eyes followed his progress on the monitor screens, watched as the Doctor opened the TARDIS door and went inside. The deep voice croaked, 'Control! Report on the molecular nature of that artefact.'

Control was the giant computer responsible for the routine operation of the ship. Its sensors were everywhere, it observed and regulated every function, so much so that the ship itself was almost a living creature.

The Doctor popped back into the control room of the TARDIS, observing with some surprise the expressions on the faces of his companions. 'Is something the matter?'

'Doctor, you're all right!' said Nyssa thankfully.

'Well, of course I'm all right.' The Doctor rubbed his

hands and looked round the little group. 'We're in motion, so we can be pretty sure we're on a spaceship.'

'So much for promises,' said Tegan bitterly. 'You've lost me my job!'

'Patience,' said the Doctor reprovingly.

'Patience!' hissed Tegan. 'If I hear that word just once more ... Men!'

Ignoring her, the Doctor said, 'But if it is a ship, it appears to be unmanned, so I think we can afford to take a look around. Adric, we'll need some more space-packs.'

'Yes, Doctor.' Adric disappeared through the inner door.

The Doctor turned to Nyssa. 'There's a lot to interest you out there, young lady. Highly advanced, innovative stuff.'

Nyssa pointed to one of the pieces of instrument-ation visible on the screen. 'That is a resonant strobo-scope, isn't it?'

'Indeed it is,' said the Doctor. 'Fascinating, isn't it?'

Adric returned with his arms full of space-packs and started passing them around.

As the others began putting the helmets on, the Doctor said, 'There seems to be nothing but machinery on this ship, but we're under observation all the same. There's a monopticon out there.'

'What's that?' asked Tegan alarmed.

The Doctor smiled. 'Well, I suppose it would be best described as a mobile black eye with a hypnotic stare. If we're being observed, that suggests an observer some-where. Whoever or whatever is running this ship knows we're here. So, we'll just go out and do a little scrutinising ourselves. If we do meet anyone, just take your cue from me.'

The Doctor opened a small compartment in the TARDIS console and took out a key. 'There you are, Tegan, spare key. If we get separated, just come back here.'

Tegan looked suspiciously at the key, making no attempt to take it. 'Why can't I just stay here?'

'All right, then, stay if you want to.' The Doctor held out the key to Adric. 'Here!'

Before Adric could take the key, Tegan had snatched it from the Doctor's hand. 'Oh no you don't,' she snapped, as if she'd caught the Doctor trying to put one over on her. 'I'm coming!'

The Doctor smiled. He'd learned by now that the best way to get Tegan to do something was to suggest the opposite. Checking that everyone's space-pack was in place and correctly adjusted, the Doctor led the way out of the TARDIS.

As soon as they stepped out into the main area the monopticon appeared, hovering inquisitively above them. The Doctor gave it another wave. 'Hello again! You must be having a ball!' Chuckling at his own awful joke, the Doctor waved a hand at his companions. 'Friends of mine.'

The monopticon made no attempt to acknowledge the introduction.

The computer voice of Control was reporting, 'Surface molecular structure of intruding artefact consistent with our planet of destination, Earth, and its solar system. The device seems screened against internal scanning.'

The three watchers absorbed the information in thoughtful silence. The Doctor brought his party to a halt in front of a particularly impressive piece of instrumentation. Tegan saw only dials, flashing lights, intertwining coils of crystalline tubings. 'Looks like an intergalactic juke-box,' she thought mutinously.

But the Doctor was clearly very impressed. 'Amazing. Absolutely amazing. Worthy of Gallifrey! Non-corrosive alloys, saturated polymers. Highly advanced!'

Nyssa indicated another equally complex piece of equipment near by. 'Look at this!'

'It's an interferometer!'

Adric was out of his technological depth. 'What's that?'

Nyssa said, 'Well, this one's for measuring gravitation waves.'

The Doctor studied it thoughtfully. 'You know, we could use this on the time-curve circuits.'

Nyssa pointed. 'And look—there's a gravitation crystal detector.'

Adric sighed. 'And what's that for?'

Nyssa smiled mischievously. 'Same thing!'

'Belt and braces?' suggested the Doctor.

'I imagine so. Except on Traken, the interferometer superceded the crystal.'

'Yes,' said the Doctor thoughtfully. 'That's what's so fascinating.'

He looked thoughtfully at the apparatus. 'It seems to be inert, Nyssa. See if you can get it going.'

Nyssa stayed by the intererometer, and the Doctor

and the others moved on.

All four were now visible on the monitor screens.

'I would look closer at the tallest,' said the deep throaty voice. 'He would appear to be the senior.'

The Doctor became aware that the hovering monopticon was moving closer to him. It seemed to be staring right into his face. The Doctor reached out to touch it. There was a slight crackle of energy, and the Doctor snatched his hand away. 'Ah, a magnetic shield. Listen, I mean you no harm. Would you mind telling me who or what you are, and where we are?'

There was no reply.

The Doctor's face filled one of the monitor screens. 'They appear to be Earthlings,' said the throaty voice. 'This one is not without intelligence or technological knowledge.'

The Doctor and his friends had reached the edge of the huge control room. There were doors set into its walls, but they were all firmly closed. Adric and Tegan tried to open them, with a complete lack of success.

The Doctor looked thoughtfully up at the monopticon. 'I know we're trespassing, but I'd like an opportunity to explain the circumstances, if you'd be so kind.'

Still no reply.

'Very well,' said the Doctor. 'Your lips are sealed. Would it be in order for you to take me to your leader.

If you have one, that is?'

Above them, one of the doors slid open. 'Now, that's a friendly gesture,' said the Doctor. He started to lead the way up the steps, and then paused. 'Perhaps one of us should stay with Nyssa. Adric?'

'No!' said Adric indignantly.

The Doctor raised his eyebrows, and somehow Adric found himself turning and heading back the way they had come.

'That's a good chap,' called the Doctor. 'We'll see you both later.'

The Doctor and Tegan went up the staircase, and through the door which closed behind them.

Adric made his way back towards Nyssa in disgust.

The monopticon bobbed along behind him. 'Go away, will you?' snarled Adric. He increased his pace, but the monopticon glided effortlessly after him.

Nyssa looked up. 'Calm down Adric, it won't bite.'

'How do you know?'

'Oh, because,' said Nyssa impatiently. 'Come over here and help me.'

Adric wandered gloomily over to her. 'I don't know why the Doctor wanted me to stay here anyway. He knows I'm no good with my hands.'

This time Adric and Nyssa were being studied on the screen. 'Their attire is interesting,' said the clear female voice. 'It obviously reflects different cultures.'

The young male voice said, 'But if they come from Earth ... How can the Earthlings have penetrated us?'

'Can they have learned the error of their ways,' suggested the female voice. 'Are they now pacified and co-operative? Is our arrival to be easier than expected?'

'More!' croaked the deep voice. 'Can their technology now be as advanced as mine?'

The Doctor and Tegan found themselves in a metal corridor, stretching endlessly into the distance. At intervals they could see doors set into the wall on either side, and junction points presumably leading to other corridors. The sheer scale of the place was astonishing, thought the Doctor. There was none of the cramped sensations so often associated with space-travel. So huge, and yet so deserted—there was something excessively grandiose about this ship, the Doctor mused. He wondered if it reflected the character of its owners.

There was another monopticon in the corridor, hanging just above their heads. The Doctor gave it his usual wave. 'Ah, a twin!'

The monopticon moved away a little, then hovered expectantly.

'I think it wants us to follow it,' said the Doctor. 'Come on, Tegan.' He set off after the monopticon. Dubiously, Tegan followed. It led them along the corridor, into another corridor and up to a door. A light came on over the door, and it slid invitingly open. 'Right you are, old fellow,' said the Doctor obligingly. 'Come along, Tegan.'

They went through the door which led into another vast corridor, much like the first.

Tegan groaned. 'How much further?'

Ignoring her, the Doctor set off after the monopticon.

Since the interferometer seemed to be a free-standing and independent unit, Nyssa's first thought was to take it into the TARDIS and work on it there. But the instrument proved to be incredibly heavy, and even with Adric's help Nyssa found it impossible to move. 'It's no good,' she gasped. 'We'll just have to take the readings out here. You do know where the time-curve circuits are, don't you, Adric?'

'Of course I do.'

'Well, fetch them out here, will you? I'll set up the apparatus.'

Giving her one of his 'Why is it always me?' looks, Adric headed for the TARDIS.

More corridors, more mysteriously opening doors, and at last the Doctor and Tegan found themselves before a set of doors larger and more impressive than any they had passed through. The doors slid open, and a kind of greenish glow spilled out from the interior. Cautiously the Doctor and Tegan moved forward. For once the monopticon did not follow, but hovered deferentially outside.

The Doctor and Tegan found themselves in an even more enormous chamber, bathed in a dim glow that gave an almost underwater effect. The high metal walls were ornately decorated with patterns and motifs that had a vaguely Egyptian feel to them. The atmosphere was like that of a temple.

No, not a temple, thought the Doctor as he looked down the length of the room. A throne room. In fact, a triple throne room.

At the far end of the room was a raised dais on which

stood three thrones, the one in the centre larger, higher and more ornately decorated than those on either side.

The occupants of the thrones were not human.

They wore ornately decorated green robes with high gold collars, and their faces were totally alien with thickly corrugated green skin and bulging eyes. They looked rather like frogs, decided the Doctor, super-intelligent technologically advanced frogs.

The creature on the centre throne was, like the throne itself, larger and more impressive than the two on either side. In a deep croaking voice it said, 'I am Monarch.'

3

The Transformation

The Doctor looked up at the massive green creature on the throne. 'Monarch, eh. Yes, you look as if you might be.'

Monarch gestured to his left. 'This is Enlightenment.'

The Doctor bowed. 'How do you do, Enlightenment?'

'How do you do?' said the creature politely. The voice was light and clear, unmistakably feminine.

Monarch gestured to his right. 'And this is Persuasion.'

'Friendly, I hope?' asked the Doctor.

Persuasion bowed his head, but did not speak.

Monarch said, 'And you are?'

'The Doctor.'

'A Doctor? Of what?' asked Enlightenment.

'Practically everything,' said the Doctor modestly.

'How modest,' said Persausion. The voice was vibrant and masculine.

Monarch persisted with his questioning, an edge of menace beneath the polite words. 'You are an Earthling?'

'A Gallifreyan. Tegan is an Earthling, Adric is an Alzarian.' The Doctor saw a picture of Nyssa on one of a row of monitor screens, set in a control console in front of the thrones. 'That's Nyssa, she is from Traken.'

'You come in peace?' asked Persuasion.

'Yes, of course. In peace, and inadvertently as a matter of fact.'

Monarch said, 'Control, release full Earth-type life-support atmosphere. Please remove your encumberances.'

Thankfully Tegan took off her helmet, and the Doctor did the same. 'Thank you. May I ask who you are?'

Monarch said proudly, 'I am the supreme ruler of the people of Urbanka in the solar system of Inokshi in the galaxy RE 1489.'

'Really? You're a long way from home.'

'So are you, Doctor,' said Monarch, still with that indefinable hint of menace. 'Yet we are both very close to Earth. You must be tired from your long journey.' He raised his voice. 'Control, refreshment for our guests.'

'You're very kind,' said the Doctor.

'I am merely civilised.'

Suddenly the creature called Enlightenment, the female, leant forward, staring at Tegan's outfit. 'Is that what the best-dressed Earthling women are wearing these days?'

'These days?'

'It is two and a half thousand years since we were last there.'

'Two thousand five hundred years?'

Monarch said loftily. 'Our planets are far apart. We

28

come as often as we can.' His bulbous eyes flicked towards the monitor. The female alien was making progress with the Interfererometer. Too much progress...
Monarch said quietly, 'Control, isolate the girl.'

The monitor screen went blank.

The sense of menace in the air was even greater now, and the Doctor began babbling to conceal his growing alarm. 'I drop in on Earth myself from time to time. Do you know, nothing on Earth changes quite so fast as their fashion in clothes. You never know what people will be wearing—mini-skirts, green hair, safety-pins ...'

Persuasion seemed puzzled. 'Safety-pins? Some defence mechanism perhaps?'

The Doctor produced a safety-pin from his pocket and held it against one ear. 'They wear them as ear-rings.'

'How barbaric!'

'Yes,' said the Doctor thoughtfully. 'There's a lot of it about.'

Enlightenment seemed strangely fascinated by the subject of clothes. 'Are you dressed fashionably, Tegan?'

'Well, not really. This is my uniform.'

'Ah yes, uniform. What is your manner of dress when not in uniform?'

'Difficult to explain,' said Tegan awkwardly. 'Got a piece of paper, Doctor?'

The Doctor fished a notebook from his pocket and handed it to her.

'Thanks,' said Tegan, taking it. 'Got a pen? Pencil?'

The Doctor handed her a handsome propelling

pencil.

Tegan started sketching.

Adric popped up from underneath the TARDIS console, looking cross and ashamed at the same time. He wasn't quite as familiar with TARDIS technology as he'd given Nyssa to understand, and the task of disconnecting the time-curve circuitry had proved quite beyond him. Maybe the TARDIS data-bank could help.

He touched a control on the console and a mini read-out screen slid into view.

Adric touched more controls and a complex circuit-diagram appeared on the screen. Adric studied it thoughtfully.

Absorbed in her work, Nyssa didn't notice when a panel in the wall opened behind her.

It was only when a shadow fell across her that Nyssa looked up, and saw the tall robed figure looming over her ...

Adric punched up another circuit diagram. It was even more baffling than the first. It was no good, he thought in annoyance, he'd have to go and ask Nyssa for help—and he'd never hear the last of that, especially if Tegan found out.

Adric marched out of the TARDIS, and into the vast control room. 'Nyssa!' he called. 'Nyssa, where are you?'

She was nowhere to be seen.

Something moved overhead. Adric looked up and

saw the monopticon. 'Well,' demanded Adric, 'where is she?'

Naturally enough, the monopticon did not reply. Instead it darted over to the door of the TARDIS, which Adric had left open in his haste. It hovered curiously outside.

'Oh no you don't,' said Adric. He dashed over to the TARDIS and slammed the door, glaring aggressively up at the monopticon.

Tegan was still sketching. Somehow the Doctor felt the atmosphere in the throne room was growing tenser by the minute.

Monarch spoke with his usual lofty courtesy. 'Is this one of your dropping times, Doctor?'

'Dropping times?'

'One of your regular visits to planet Earth.'

'Well, not really. I promised to get Tegan on her plane.'

'Her astral plane?'

'Not exactly. The kind of plane that leaves from Heathrow.'

'This is not Heathrow.'

'No, it isn't,' said the Doctor sadly. 'Not even the quarantine area.'

With a kind of steely politeness, Monarch persisted in his interrogation. 'Forgive my curiosity—but how did your craft come aboard?'

'By error,' said the Doctor simply. 'My assistant miscalculated the co-ordinates.'

Tegan glanced up briefly from her sketching. 'Too

right he did.'

'Just a simple error, you see,' said the Doctor. 'Or, of course, it could have been your intense magnetic field causing a fluctuation of my artron energy.'

Monarch leaned forward eagerly. 'What energy is that?'

Adric watched the monopticon glide across the control area and halt above a door at the far end. A light came on above the door, and it slid open.

'Follow my leader, is it?' said Adric. 'All right, then, off we go!' He went through the door and into the corridor, the monopticon gliding encouragingly ahead of him.

'Come now, Doctor,' said Monarch reprovingly. 'Do you really mean to tell me that you possess an energy you do not understand?'

'Silly, isn't it?' said the Doctor cheerfully. 'Only my professor at the Academy really seemed to understand artron energy. Just shows how academic everything is, doesn't it?'

Monarch treated the feeble joke with the contempt it deserved. He frowned, and leant forward, about to pursue the questioning, when there was a welcome distraction.

A wall panel opened and Adric stepped into the control room.

'Ah,' said Monarch expansively. 'The boy who got his sums wrong.'

'I didn't,' said Adric indignantly. 'I'm a mathematician.'

Monarch gave a throaty chuckle. 'A mathematician, are you? Tell me, what do you understand by $E = MC^2$?'

Adric was looking around. 'Where's Nyssa?'

That point was concerning the Doctor too, but he didn't want to show it, not yet. 'Come on, Adric, explain the formula.'

'Where's Nyssa?'

The Doctor shot him a warning glance. 'The formula, Adric!'

'Energy equals mass times the speed of light squared,' said Adric.

Monarch seemed astonished. 'You grasp the theory of relativity?'

'Doesn't everyone?'

Tegan had finished her sketching. 'Well, I don't.' She glared accusingly at the Doctor. 'And if I don't get to London airport in time I shall lose my job.'

'Study maths and you might get a better one,' said Adric unsympathetically.

'I don't want a better one!'

'Children, children,' said the Doctor reprovingly. 'Not in front of our ... hosts, please.'

Angrily Tegan ripped a couple of pages from the Doctor's notebook and shoved pencil and book back at him. She glanced uncertainly at the three enthroned aliens, wondering what to do with the sketches.

Enlightenment leaned forward, extending a four-clawed hand. The Doctor took the drawings from Tegan and passed them to Enlightenment, glancing at them as he did so. Tegan had drawn rather idealised portraits of a handsome young man in flowing slacks and a tailored blazer, and a girl in an elegant dress and

33

fashionably high boots.

Enlightenment took the drawings and passed them to Monarch, who studied them for a moment. 'Thank you, Doctor. You will be escorted to your refreshment.'

A door close to the Doctor slid open. Taking the hint, the Doctor bowed. 'Thank you, Monarch.'

'Majesty,' corrected Monarch reprovingly.

'Of course, Majesty,' said the Doctor hurriedly, and ushered Adric and Tegan through the door. It closed behind them.

Monarch rose, handing the drawings back to Enlightenment. 'Well done, Enlightenment. These will eliminate the need for telemicrographics, and may well be more reliable.'

He descended the steps of the dais. 'I would inspect their craft.'

Guided as before by a monopticon, the Doctor and his two companions walked along yet another corridor. 'What about Nyssa, Doctor?'

The Doctor glanced up at the monopticon and said in a loud cheerful voice. 'Nyssa? I'm sure she's in good hands.'

The monopticon stopped over a door which duly slid open.

'Thank you,' said the Doctor and led his companions inside.

They found themselves in a large empty room—with Nyssa standing alone in the centre. 'You see?' said the Doctor. 'What did I tell you?'

Adric hurried over to her. 'Are you all right?'

'Just about.'

The Doctor was looking around the room. It seemed to be some kind of leisure area. It was furnished with a variety of tables and couches and chairs, and the walls were decorated with a variety of frescoes and murals, in a strange mixture of styles, an odd mingling of Mayan, Chinese and classical Greek.

The Doctor glanced up at the hovering monopticon. By now it almost seemed like an old friend. 'Still here, are you? That's reassuring!'

Monarch rattled angrily at the door of the TARDIS with a four-fingered green hand. After a moment he stepped back and ordered, 'Laser key!'

A nozzle slid out from a nearby console and a pencil of brilliant purple light shot out striking the TARDIS lock. The ray cut out and Monarch tried the door again. It was still locked.

'Directional cobalt flux,' ordered Monarch angrily.

Another nozzle appeared and a deep blue ray, thicker this time, flung itself against the TARDIS lock in fierce pulses of energy. This too cut out. Monarch tried the door once more. It was still shut fast.

Angrily he crashed his fist against the side of the TARDIS. 'This artefact is too primitive to defy my technology!'

The TARDIS door remained obstinately closed.

'This person who brought you here, Nyssa,' said the Doctor. 'What was he like?'

'Well, he was human, humanoid anyway—' Nyssa broke off as a door slid open. 'See for yourself, Doctor.'

A man was standing in the doorway.

The man was tall, white-haired and white-bearded, and he wore a simple linen robe. He was carrying a long metal tray. He came forward into the room, and placed the tray on a nearby table. 'Welcome. My name is Bigon.'

'Well, he looks human enough,' said Tegan.

'How do you do?' said the Doctor politely. 'I'm the Doctor, this is Tegan, Adric, and this is Nyssa.'

'We've already met,' said Nyssa.

'Are you an Earthling, Bigon?' asked the Doctor.

'Yes.'

'Greek?'

Bigon nodded. 'I am an Athenian.'

'What are you doing here?'

As if the question had not registered, Bigon said calmly, 'Will it please you to eat and drink?'

The Doctor and his companions took their places around the table.

Bigon indicated the tray which was divided into a number of compartments. 'A simple meal ... citrus fruits, apples, nuts, avocado pears, and grape juice.'

Adric picked up an avocado. 'It's a small river-fruit!'

'It is an avocado pear,' said Bigon gravely. 'It is best eaten with a pinch of sodium chloride.'

'What?'

'Salt!' said the Doctor.

Adric grinned. 'Pass the sodium chloride, then!'

The Doctor passed him a small container. 'Bigon, if you're an Earthling, how do you come to be —' He broke off as an extraordinary figure came into the room.

The newcomer was dark-skinned, broad-shouldered,

dressed only in a headband and loincloth. His body was painted with black and yellow stripes.

Tegan stared at the newcomer in astonishment, and then spoke to him, a string of deep gutteral syllables.

The man smiled and responded in what was obviously the same tongue.

The Doctor stared at Tegan in astonishment. 'You speak his language?'

'He's an Australian, like me—an Australian Aborigine!'

'Yes, I know,' said the Doctor impatiently. 'What's he saying?'

'His name is Kurkutji. He welcomes us in Peace.'

'Ask him what he's doing here.'

'I was asking him!'

'Sorry to interrupt,' said the Doctor wearily. 'Well, ask him again.'

There was another brief interchange between Tegan and Kurkutji in the same gutteral tongue, then Tegan said, 'He says he's going walkabout, to the time of the dreaming.'

'The dreaming?'

'Heaven. He says we're all going to heaven.'

In his throne room, Monarch could see and hear everything that took place. He chuckled throatily at Tegan's reply. 'As I have always said, "Out of the mouths of primates and primitives ..." '

'So when does he expect to get to Heaven?' asked the Doctor.

Tegan shrugged. 'He doesn't seem very sure. Doctor, I'm frightened.'

'So am I,' said Nyssa quietly.

The Doctor turned to Bigon. 'Is that where you're going—Heaven?'

Bigon shook his head. 'I am not a believer.'

'No, of course you're not.'

An olive-skinned woman in ornate ceremonial robes came into the room. Her elaborate head-dress and the ceremonial jewels she wore suggested some kind of priestess.

'Allow me to introduce the Princess Villagra,' said Bigon.

The Doctor bowed. 'How do you do, your Highness?'

The Princess nodded graciously, and passed on without speaking.

Bigon said quietly. 'The Princess has vowed not to talk again till she is reunited with her people.'

The Doctor looked curiously after the exotic figure. 'What people?'

'The Mayan people of the Americas.'

'That's going back a bit.'

Yet another Earthling entered the room, this time a tall man with a round cheerful face and a neatly trimmed moustache, wearing a quilted robe and the traditional topknot of the Chinese mandarin. He bowed his head. 'Greetings!'

The Doctor returned the bow. 'Greetings!'

'I am Lin Futu.'

'I'd never have guessed it. You look in the best of health to me.'

Either the Mandarin failed to understand the

Doctor's joke, or he was polite enough to ignore it. He bowed again and said, 'Thank you.'

The Doctor looked round the strangely assorted group. 'You're all from Earth. What are you doing on this ship?'

No one replied.

'Are you all hostages—is that it?'

In the throne room Monarch said, 'Tell them nothing.'

Bigon seemed about to speak, then checked himself. 'You have not been told by Monarch?'

'No.'

'Then we must be silent on this.'

Two more Earthlings, a man and a woman, both tall and elegantly handsome, had entered the room, both wearing the kind of clothes fashionable in the 1980s.

Tegan stared at them in astonishment, wondering why they looked so familiar. Then she realised. The man's blazer, the girl's long dress and high boots—they were wearing the clothes she had sketched in the throne room.

Even the faces were like those in her drawing.

In a clear, pleasant voice, which also seemed familiar, the woman said, 'His Majesty commands me to tell you that we arrive on planet Earth in four days. He invites you to complete your journey as his guests.'

'That's very civil of his Majesty,' said the Doctor. He had the feeling that the invitation was one which it would be impossible to refuse. 'And who are you?'

The man said, 'We have already met, Doctor, in the throne room. This is Enlightenment, and I am Persuasion.'

4

The Invaders

The Doctor looked at the two elegant figures with astonishment, remembering the form in which he had last seen them, the frog-like features and green corrugated skin. 'My, how you've changed!'

It was not surprising that they should be able to copy the clothes in Tegan's drawing, but to copy the human bodies which wore them ...

Tegan was still taking in the astonishing transformation. 'But you're what I sketched!'

Enlightenment smiled. 'Yes. You are an excellent draughtswoman, my dear.'

Tegan edged closer to the Doctor. 'I want to go.'

'There is no need to be frightened,' said Enlightenment calmly. 'Please stay.'

'I'm not frightened,' muttered Tegan defiantly. But she was.

Adric was staring at the two tall elegant figures in awe. 'How did you do it—just change like that?'

'We enjoy the most advanced technology in the universe.' There was a hint of complacency in Enlightenment's voice.

'Magical,' said the Doctor politely.

'No, not magic, Doctor. A skill, like any other.'

Adric stared at her. 'You mean anyone can do it?'

'Yes.'

'Even me?'

'If you wished,' said Enlightenment placidly. 'But you have no need. Yet.'

'But you have?' asked the Doctor casually.

'As you have seen, Doctor. Earthlings find our native form ... disturbing.'

Persuasion said smoothly, 'The dominant emotion on planet Earth is fear. When last we were there, our reception was hostile.'

'That doesn't surprise me,' said Tegan, remembering the sinister frog-like creatures on the three thrones.

'We must read your history books,' said the Doctor brightly.

Enlightenment inclined her head. 'You will be welcome to do so. It will also be necessary for me to instruct you in our computer language.'

'One couldn't wish for a more charming teacher.'

Persuasion said, 'A very elevated one, Doctor.'

'Yes, indeed. Enlightenment herself!'

'*Minister* of Enlightenment.'

'Yes, of course.' The Doctor looked thoughtfully at him. 'And you? Now, let me guess ... Minister of Persuasion?'

In his throne room Monarch growled, 'Control, a close watch on this Monarch. Report what may be known of this being. Report also on "Gallifrey" and on "Artron Energy".'

'And may we know the purpose of your visit to planet Earth?'

'Resettlement, Doctor,' said Persuasion calmly.

'Urbanka, our native planet, no longer exists,' explained Enlightenment. 'Inokshi, our sun was an irregular variable.'

Curious, thought the Doctor, how they spoke alternately, almost as if both voices came from the same brain.

Now it was Persuasion's turn. 'Our people left before the end.'

Then Enlightenment: 'In time to escape the black hole.'

'Were there many of you?' asked the Doctor innocently.

Enlightenment said, 'Three billion.'

'Three billion?' gasped Adric. 'On how many ships?'

'One,' said Enlightenment. 'This one.'

Monarch leaned forward on his throne. 'They have been told enough.'

The voice of Control said, 'Data on Doctor, Gallifrey, Artron energy not memory-banked. Inference, fifth dimension.'

'This Doctor cannot have brought mathematics further than I. Infer again!'

'The occult.'

'Superstition? No! Isolate them. I must know more about them.'

There came a faint hum from the monopticon. Instantly Enlightenment said, 'Now that you are refreshed, Doctor, you must see your quarters. Bigon will show you. He was the last to use them.'

'I see. We've accepted your invitation, have we?'

Enlightenment smiled. 'Most graciously.'

The Doctor bowed. 'Of course.'

Bigon moved to a door which slid open before him. 'This way, if you please.'

The Doctor looked round the room, at Enlightenment, Persuasion, and at the strangely assorted group of Earthmen. '*Au revoir*, then?'

Enlightenment smiled. 'I hope so, Doctor.'

Tegan shivered.

Bigon led them along more corridors and finally into a large and well-lit room. Like the recreation area it was simply but comfortably furnished. There were chairs and couches and low tables, and along the walls a number of built-in bunk beds.

'Here, you will be comfortable,' said Bigon placidly. 'As I was.'

'Where are the others?' asked Adric. 'The rest of the three billion?'

'I am sure that Monarch, or one of his ministers, will wish to satisfy your curiosity.'

The Doctor looked round the comfortable room. 'I do hope we're not turning you out?'

'No. I have no need of this accomodation now.'

'You're with your family?'

'I have no family. Not since I was rescued from Earth a hundred generations ago.'

'Why does the old fool have to chatter so?' snarled Monarch.

The hovering monopticon buzzed, and Bigon said, 'I must leave you now.'

The door slid closed behind him.

Tegan rushed to try and open it, without success. 'We're shut in.'

Adric shook his head in awe. 'A hundred generations!'

'Looks young for his age, doesn't he?' said the Doctor, fishing in his pockets for his sonic screwdriver.

'Three billion people!' said Adric. 'How big is this ship?'

'Not that big,' said Nyssa. 'It's impossible.'

The Doctor found his sonic screwdriver and began taking a number of readings around the chamber. 'Yes, on the face of it.'

Tegan was beginning to panic. 'I want to get out of here. I want to be off this ship. I don't want to be "rescued" for a hundred generations, like Bigon.' She turned to the Doctor. 'Can you get us out of here? Can you get us back to the TARDIS?'

'I don't expect a great deal of difficulty.'

'Then I want to leave, Doctor. Now!'

The Doctor was still prowling around the room. 'There was a sailor once,' he said vaguely. 'Friend of mine named Drake.'

'What's he got to do with it?'

'He said something like, "There's plenty of time to get to Heathrow Airport, and beat the Armada too!" '

In the throne room, Monarch had been joined by Enlightenment and Persuasion, still in their human forms. Monarch sat between them, glowering at the monitor screen which showed the Doctor and his companions in their new quarters.

'This Doctor interests me more and more. On no account is he to be allowed to leave.'

With a sudden gesture, the Doctor swept the hat from his head and dropped it on top of the hovering monopticon. He whipped his sonic screwdriver from his pocket and made a swift adjustment, aiming it at the monopticon. The monopticon hovered, blinded, humming uneasily. The Doctor moved his hat, made another adjustment. The monopticon started to spin.

The same fluctuating hum could be heard in the throne room, and one of Monarch's monitor screens was blank.

'He has blocked the picture, and the sound,' said Monarch almost admiringly. 'Here we have a lively intelligence. He could be a valuable ally.'

Persuasion frowned. 'Or a dangerous enemy, your Majesty?'

'He is too jocular,' said Enlightenment disapprovingly.

'He is irresponsible. Such a being prefers mental anarchy. He would call it freedom.'

Monarch glared at them. 'You speak nonsense, both of you. I have eliminated the concept of opposition.'

'What of Bigon, your Majesty?' asked Persuasion.

'Bigon cannot oppose.'

'But he does not conform.'

'Naturally. He is a philospher. A doubter. We need doubt, it is the greatest intellectual galvaniser. That is why Bigon is permitted a measure of free will.'

'With respect, your Majesty,' said Enlightenment almost timidly, 'there is a sensitivity in his persona which suggests what in the Flesh Time was called ...' she hesitated '... *soul*.'

Monarch was outraged. 'This is the first time, Enlightenment, that I have heard you blaspheme.'

Enlightenment bowed her head. 'I beg your Majesty's pardon.'

'I should think so,' said Monarch severely. 'Soul, indeed! I have abolished soul!'

The whining of the monopticon was beginning to get on Tegan's nerves. 'Must you make that awful noise, Doctor?'

'If our conversation is to remain private, yes!'

Adric was still brooding over Enlightenment's amazing claim. 'Three billion people, in one ship! It would never get off the ground. They must be lying—or mad!'

Tegan was inclined to agree with him. 'Of course they're mad. A hundred generations, in this thing? They've got to be mad.'

'She didn't talk of people,' said the Doctor thoughtfully. 'She spoke of population.'

'Same thing.'

'Sloppy thinking, young Adric. There are more than three billion bacteria in this chamber alone. And if a frog with a funny hairdo can turn itself into a semblance of a human being in a matter of minutes, there can't be much limit to what else it can do . . . to say nothing of the dressmaking!'

'All that's not so difficult,' said Tegan defiantly.

Adric shook his head. 'Not difficult, she says!'

Nyssa gave Tegan a reproving look. 'You have to face it, these Urbankans are terribly advanced.'

Tegan sighed. 'Terribly's just the word.'

'They've reached a level far beyond me,' Nyssa went on. 'And I like to think I'm an expert in bioengineering and cybernetics.'

'What's cybernetics?'

'The science of machine control mechanisms.'

Nyssa's reply left Tegan very little the wiser. 'What machines? I've seen three large frogs and four very peculiar people.'

'You've seen more than that. You saw two sketches—sketches you made yourself—come to life!'

'Don't remind me.'

'I'm sure that, somehow or other, what we saw was done by machine.'

'Come on, we're talking about flesh and blood—' began Tegan.

The Doctor interrupted her. 'You know, I've been wondering . . . we're four days from Earth, in a spaceship with three billion and three frogs and four Earthlings. Why?' He began pacing up and down. 'Wait a minute, wait a minute . . .' He turned to Adric. 'How long is one hundred generations?'

'What's a generation?'

'Call it twenty-five years.'

'Two thousand five hundred years, then. Why?'

'Right! It's two thousand five hundred years since our hosts were last on earth. How's your ancient history, Tegan?'

'In the same state as I am—awful!'

'Not to worry,' said the Doctor cheerfully. 'Mine's pretty good! Now, the Futu dynasty in China ... I'd place that about four thousand years ago. The Mayans flourished in South America about eight thousand years ago. That Aborigine, Kurkutji, says it's so long since he was taken he can't remember. So, let's say twelve thousand years.'

'That's mad,' said Tegan flatly.

'Yes, so you keep saying, Tegan. Who's disagreeing with you?'

'I am,' said Adric. 'I think it's brilliant.'

'So do I,' said Nyssa. 'Pure logic, Doctor!'

Tegan was still baffled. 'Are you telling me that Aborigine was taken from Earth twelve thousand years ago?'

'Well, no! But his ancestors could have been. It wouldn't be the first time whole generations knew no other world but a spaceship.'

'Just what are you suggesting, Doctor?'

'I'm suggesting that these Urbankans have visited Earth at least four times and "rescued" at least one cultural representative each time. Maybe more than one, for all we know. This time they're coming for good. An invasion.' The Doctor stared into space as if foreseeing some unimaginable horror. 'Three billion Earthlings, *plus* three billion Urbankans? I don't think so. I don't think so at all. We've got to stop them.'

5

The Explorers

Adric stared blankly at the Doctor. 'Stop them? Us? What can we do?'

The Doctor waved his sonic screwdriver. 'Explore!'

Monarch, Enlightenment and Persuasion were staring at the still-blank monitor screen.

Persuasion looked anxiously at Monarch. 'What action shall we take, your Majesty?'

Monarch gave one of his throaty chuckles. 'Action? None! The Doctor will take the action.' Monarch gestured towards the screen. 'He is using a sonic device, primitive but effective. Now he will want to explore.' Monarch brooded for a moment. 'Arrange for a recreational to divert our friend! And separate him from the boy and girl. I wish to speak to them alone. They will tell me more about this Doctor than he will himself!'

At the end of a few minutes concentrated work, the closed door had surrendered to the Doctor's sonic screwdriver. The Doctor stood back as the door slid open, and went to pick up his space-pack. 'Come on, all of you. And bring these!'

Gathering up their space-packs, Adric, Nyssa and Tegan followed him out into the corridor.

Another monopticon bobbed after them. The Doctor looked up at it. 'Don't suppose you'd care to show us around?' The Doctor was well aware that there was no hope of his escape going undetected. Testing the Urbankan's reaction was very much part of his plan. In fact, you might almost say it was the whole of his plan. The Doctor, as usual, was poking his nose into things, and hoping that some solution would present itself. It usually did, in the end.

The Urbankans' first reaction came very quickly. A door ahead of the Doctor lit up and slid open. The Doctor strode through it, followed by Tegan, and the door promptly slid shut in Adric's face. The party had been neatly divided.

Nyssa looked at Adric. 'What shall we do now?'

Further down the huge corridor, another door lit up and slid open.

Adric sighed. 'Come on!'

In the throne room Monarch smiled benevolently. 'Let them move freely—for the time being. In the meantime, Enlightenment, I would examine Bigon.'

'At once, your Majesty.'

Fully at home in her new human form, Enlightenment moved gracefully from the room.

On a monitor, Monarch could see Adric and Nyssa making their way cautiously down the corridor. He smiled.

The Doctor heard the sound of distant music and

began striding hopefully towards it.

Tegan tugged at his sleeve. 'Doctor, we've lost the others.'

'So we have.'

He went back to the door that had cut them off and worked on it for a few moments with his sonic screwdriver. Nothing happened. 'Mmm! I have a feeling we were meant to lose them!'

'But we can't just leave them!'

'What do you suggest? Come on, Tegan, and try to keep calm. We'll get nowhere if you keep losing your head!'

The Doctor set off again. Shooting a look of burning reproach at his retreating back, Tegan followed.

The corridor led them to another door, which led them onto a kind of gallery, not unlike the dress circle in a cinema or theatre. In this case the gallery ran round all four sides of a huge, high-ceilinged hall. The big open space in the centre had more seats arranged around it, and was clearly designed for performances and exhibitions.

At the moment, four aborigines wearing loincloths and paint were solemnly dancing to the strains of a kind of low-tuned instrument played by Kurkutji, the Aborigine they had encountered earlier.

'It's one of their tribal dances,' whispered Tegan. 'He's playing a didgeridoo!'

'So there are more Earthlings on board. It looks as if someone's arranged some entertainment for us.'

Below them, watching from the side of the hall they could see Villagra, the Mayan princess, and a group of similarly dressed handmaidens. There was a scattering of other humans too, wearing a costume that the Doctor identified as ancient Greek.

The Chinese mandarin Lin Futu was there as well with a little group of his fellow mandarins.

The Doctor was studying the colourful and exotically dressed group thoughtfully, and something caught his eye. All the Earthlings seemed to be wearing a broad metal strip about their wrists. All that is, except those he had already met, like the mandarin Lin Futu, Princess Villagra, and Kurkutji the Aborigine.

The Doctor was speculating about the wristband's possible function when he saw the elegant figure of Persuasion coming along the gallery towards them.

'Welcome to our recreational, Doctor.'

'Thank you.'

The tall young man glanced at Tegan, and then looked round in elaborate surprise. 'But where are your two other companions?'

'I'm afraid they wandered off and got lost. You know what children are.'

The young man smiled coldly. 'I don't, as it happens. But do not concern yourself, Doctor. They won't get far.'

Tegan shivered. There was a sinister undertone to the words, and there was something very odd about this elegantly handsome young man. The fact that, in a way, she'd created him didn't seem to help at all.

Persuasion waved a hand at the colourful scene in the hall below. 'We have these recreationals from time to time. It forms a diversion from work and study, and of course it is representative of the many different cultures amongst us.'

'And how is Urbanka represented?'

Persuasion looked up sharply at the Doctor's question. 'We have no comparable rituals. Such concepts are essentially for the primitive.' There was a chilling contempt in his voice.

The dance continued.

Calm and unruffled as ever, Bigon knelt before Monarch upon his throne.

Monarch pointed a threatening claw at the calm, white-bearded figure of the old philosopher. 'Bigon, you must resist the temptation to tell this Doctor about my mission.'

'I cannot lie,' said Bigon simply. 'I have been telling the truth for over two and a half thousand years.'

'Then keep silent!' snarled Monarch. 'You haven't been made immortal to engage in endless gossip. I want to know a great deal more about this Doctor before I tell him of the Ultimate.'

'When you do tell him, his hand will be against you.'

'Then I shall cut it off!'

'We cannot find the Ultimate,' continued Bigon calmly. 'There is no Ultimate to find.'

'Hold your tongue,' snapped Monarch. 'I have heard more than enough blasphemy for one day. If it were not for me, you would still be thinking your Earth was flat. It will be time for the Doctor to know more about us when we know more about him. Now leave us.'

Bigon rose, bowed and walked placidly from the throne room.

Adric and Nyssa meanwhile, after wandering in what

seemed like endless corridors, had suddenly found themselves in a jungle.

It was of course an indoor jungle, a kind of tropical greenhouse. Light that felt as bright and as warm as sunshine streamed down from some hidden source high overhead. There were plants everywhere, rows upon rows of them: grapevines and avocados, lush shrubs and grasses, and exotic plants, even full-grown tropical trees.

The area was divided by walkways, and here and there figures could be seen tending the vegetation. They were Aborigines, like Karkutji, and they all wore plain metal wristbands.

Adric blinked. 'Why do they keep this light so bright?'

'Photosynthesis,' said Nyssa. 'The light on the plants converts carbon dioxide into carbohydrate and the plants give off oxygen.'

They wandered along the pathways and came up to one of the Aborigines, who seemed to be re-planting a shrub.

'Hello,' said Adric cheerfully.

The Aborigine ignored him. Adric shrugged and moved on to join Nyssa, who had discovered a little pool hidden amidst the luxuriant green vegetation.

At its edge several frogs were basking in the artificial sunshine, croaking contentedly.

The Aboriginal war dance came to an end at last, and there was a brief pattering of polite applause.

Linu Futu struck a Chinese gong, and as its notes echoed around the chamber, a traditional Chinese

dragon pranced in. In reality a huge costume conceal-
ing several men, the dragon wound its way around the
huge chamber, weaving some kind of ceremonial
dance.

Tegan nudged the Doctor. 'Shouldn't we look for the
others?'

'No need. As our friend Percy Persuasion over there
said, they can't be far.'

'Suppose this Urbankan lot harm them?'

'Why should they?'

'I don't know,' said Tegan exasperatedly. 'I just think
they will!'

The Doctor seemed absorbed by the caperings of the
dragon. 'Nonsense. Harming them just wouldn't make
any sense.'

'It doesn't have to make sense. I think they're mad . . .
and I think you're mad too!'

The Doctor smiled. 'In that case, take some good
advice from a madman. Look happy!'

'What?'

'In a situation like this, it's the best form of defence . . . and it gives me time to think.'

Adric and Nyssa left the plant area, travelled more
corridors and went through another door, and found
themselves in a very different environment. It was a
huge computer room, its walls lined with row upon row
of data-banks. Scattered about the room were a
number of free-standing computer terminals, and
working at their keyboards were calm robed figures
much like the old Greek philosopher Bigon. The place

had the hushed and peaceful atmosphere of a university library.

As they studied the busy scene, Adric suddenly became aware of something: he couldn't breathe.

Monarch, watching on his monitor, smiled grimly.

Calmly, Enlightenment studied the gasping pair on the screen. 'They have lungs.'

'Then let them remember that!'

Adric held up his space-pack to Nyssa and pulled it over his head. Nyssa did the same with hers.

'Not enough oxygen,' gasped Adric. He looked at the calmly working scholars. 'Not that they seem to need any.'

Adric went over to the nearest. 'Excuse me!'

The robed figure ignored him.

Adric touched the scholar's bare forearm, just above the wristband, and then jerked his hand away. 'He's ice-cold!'

Nyssa came over to join him. She reached out and touched the wristband. 'Have you noticed, they all seem to be wearing these things.'

The scholar glanced up, looking calmly at her, but made no attempt to resist her examination.

When Nyssa released his arm, he continued with his work as though neither of them existed.

Eventually the dragon dance wound its way to an end, and just as it did so Bigon made his way onto the gallery.

Two men appeared in the central area, both tall and

muscular, wearing the brief kilt-like garments and the leather harness of Greek warriors. They carried round shields and short stabbing swords.

They began to fight.

Bigon edged closer to the Doctor and said quietly, 'I wish it to appear that I am explaining the contest to you.' He glanced across at Persuasion, who was watching them keenly.

The Doctor looked down at the feinting, thrusting warriors below and nodded eagerly. 'Go on.'

Bigon said quietly, 'I must see you in private as soon as possible.'

'I fancy I've made our quarters private enough.'

'Excellent. Could you divert the attention of the monopticon for a small space of time?'

The Doctor looked up. As always one of the metal globes was hovering close at hand. 'I'll do my best.'

'In ten seconds then, please.' Bigon moved away, and stood near the exit, apparently absorbed in the contest below.

The Doctor turned to Tegan. 'Be sure to act up to me!

Suddenly he collapsed in his seat, sliding unconscious to the floor.

6

The Android

Quite genuinely surprised, Tegan shouted, 'Doctor!' She knelt beside him. 'Doctor, what's the matter?' And while the monopticon focused on the Doctor and Tegan, Bigon meanwhile slipped quietly from the gallery.

Persuasion moved over to them. 'Are you not well, Doctor?'

The Doctor opened his eyes, struggled to his feet, and then sat down in his chair. 'Perfectly all right, thank you. Just a sudden dizzy spell.' He grinned weakly. 'It must be the altitude!'

Monarch and Enlightenment were studying the Doctor on the monitor. Enlightenment said wonderingly, 'What a fatuous remark! Can he really be intelligent?'

Monarch shook his head. 'Ah, the Flesh Time! The Flesh Time!'

Adric and Nyssa had passed through the computer room, along more corridors and into another area that looked like a kind of hospital. Shelves all around held row upon row of gleaming cylinders. In the centre of the room was a kind of operating table, with a huge plastic dome suspended above it. On the table was the body of a man. Two robed mandarins, very much like Lin Futu, stood over him. They seemed to be fitting a metal band on his wrist. They finished and the man rose and walked away.

There was something very sinister about the scene.

'I don't suppose it's any use talking to this lot either,' whispered Adric.

'I very much doubt it.' Nyssa pointed. 'Look, there's an electron microscope.'

Adric looked, then pointed to another bulkier piece of equipment close by. 'And what's this?'

'Looks like an induction furnace.'

They wandered around the room, studying the equipment, ignored by the two Chinamen, who worked steadily at their various tasks.

This too was visible on the monitor in the throne room.

Enlightenment said, 'Your Majesty, is it wise to let them see the Mobilliary?'

'Do you question my wisdom, Enlightenment?' There was astonishment in Monarch's voice.

'Naturally not, your Majesty. But they will communicate what they have seen to their companions—and to the Doctor.'

'Of course,' said Monarch complacently. 'But I intend to control and qualify that communication!'

Their tour of the chamber completed, Adric looked helplessly at Nyssa. 'What's going on? What do they do in here?'

Nyssa glanced up at the hovering monopticon, and shook her head very slightly.

In the recreation hall, the duel between the two Greek warriors was reaching its climax.

The Doctor watched without too much interest, expecting the contest to end in some ritualised mime representing the death of one of the warriors and the triumph of the other.

There was a sudden flurry of action down below, a series of fierce blows and parries—and suddenly one of the warriors lunged. It was a classic killing blow, transfixing his opponent just below the sternum. So forceful was the thrust that the sword blade could be seen projecting from the defeated warrior's back—just below the tenth thoracic vertebra, noted the Doctor automatically.

Beside him Tegan gave a gasp of horror, leapt to her feet and hurried from the room.

The sword was withdrawn—curiously enough, no blood was visible—and the victim slumped to the floor. There was more applause, loud and enthusiastic this time. Evidently killing was a more popular form of amusement than folk-dancing, reflected the Doctor.

The victor raised his sword in a salute of triumph. Two more warriors entered, lifted the fallen man and carried him away. Then the Mayan handmaidens came into the centre of the room and began an elegant ceremonial dance.

The Doctor rose and went off after Tegan.

Still in the surgery, Nyssa and Adric watched in

puzzlement as what appeared to be a severely wounded Greek warrior walked unaided into the room, followed by a second, who carried the wounded man's sword and shield, as well as his own. The wounded man lay down on the operating table.

Nyssa gasped at the sight of the terrible wound. 'He ought to be dead!'

The transparent dome was lowered over the Warrior's body, and one of the robed figures went to a bank of controls. The dome was suddenly filled with pulsing light. The light faded, the dome was lifted ... and the warrior swung his legs down from the table, taking his sword and shield from his waiting companion. The terrible wound in his body had completely vanished.

Nyssa looked at Adric. 'So that's what they do in here!'

In the throne room Monarch growled, 'Enough! Bring those children to me!'

In the Mobilliary there was a sudden buzz from the hovering monopticon. Suddenly the two warriors advanced menacingly on Adric and Nyssa.

They backed away, but by now the mandarins were closing in on them from the other side. There was no escape.

In the Doctor's quarters, Bigon was talking to the

Doctor and Tegan. As always, he spoke the truth because this was his nature. The story he had to tell was utterly terrifying.

When Bigon had finished, Tegan said, 'It looks as if you were right, Doctor. It is an invasion.'

'Yes, of course I was right,' said the Doctor modestly. 'Four visits, about every four thousand years or so? That's it, isn't it, Bigon?'

'No, Doctor. The first visit was thirty-five thousand years ago, when Kurkutji was taken. It took twenty thousand years for the Urbankans to reach Earth.'

'But surely ...'

'Monarch has doubled the speed of the ship on every subsequent visit,' said Bigon simply.

Tegan had been struggling with mental arithmetic. 'Then you last left Urbanka—what? Twelve hundred and fifty years ago?'

'That is so.'

'How do they manage to make organic life endure s[o] long?' asked the Doctor.

Bigon gave a melancholy smile. 'There is no organ[ic] life on board, Doctor—at least, only in the Fl[o]Chamber.'

'Are you trying to tell me—'

Bigon slipped his robe from his shoulders, revea[ling] a rather scrawny bare chest. He opened his chest, [like] someone unfastening an invisible zip, peeling bac[k] skin to reveal—nothing. Empty space. It was [as if] Bigon was constructed around some kind of h[ollow] framework.

Unfastening his skin at the throat, Bigon lifted [off] his entire face, revealing the same terrifying blan[k]

65

'This compound is not me,' said Bigon's voice.

He reached inside his chest cavity, and then held out his hand. In his palm the Doctor and Tegan saw three tiny pieces of circuitry.

Bigon said sadly: 'This is me.'

7

The Convert

The placid voice came out of that terrifying blankness, and a bony finger touched each of the chips in turn. 'This is my memory of two thousand five hundred and fifty-five years. It is linked to this, which is my reason, and that, which is my motor power.'

Bigon replaced the chips inside his chest cavity, lifted the peeled-back skin into place and became once again the gentle old philosopher they had first encountered. 'This compound is a polymer, stretched on a non-corrosive metal frame.'

Even the Doctor was impressed. 'What incredible engineering!'

'No,' breathed Tegan. 'It's wicked, evil ...'

Bigon shook his head. 'Not in itself. As with all technology, the good or evil lies in the use to which it is put.'

'Quite so,' said the Doctor. 'All the same, it's pretty amazing what can be done with just three silicon chips.'

'My reasoning chip has more circuits than there are synapses in your brain, Doctor. They are linked by lines one hundred nanometers thick.' Bigon spoke with a kind of melancholy pride.

'Doctor, what's a nanometer?' whispered Tegan.

'What? Oh, a thousand-millionths of a metre,' said the Doctor absently.

Tegan shook her head. 'I'm sorry, I just don't believe all this. I've seen it, but I still don't believe it!'

The Doctor waved a hand towards Bigon. 'Whether you like it or not, Tegan, you're looking at a fact, if not exactly a fact of life. This ship carries the entire population of Urbanka. Nine billion silicon chips.'

Bigon shook his head. 'Not nearly so many, Doctor. Some are slaves, robots if you will. They have but one chip, the motor circuits.'

Suddenly the Doctor understood. 'I see. And those are the ones who wear those bracelet-things?'

'That is so.'

'The mandarin, Lin Futu, and Kurkutji the Aborigine, and that Mayan princess—they're all like you? The superior version, complete personalities reproduced on silicon chips, housed in immortal mechanical bodies?'

'That is so, Doctor. Those you speak of are all as I am. We are the leaders of our ethnic groups.'

Tegan said, 'Now hang on a minute. Are you telling me these Urbankans have turned the people they took from Earth into robots?'

'And themselves too, Tegan,' the Doctor pointed out. 'That's how Enlightenment and Persuasion were able to change. They had new clothes and new bodies made, and put themselves, their essences, into them.'

'I just don't believe it,' said Tegan again. She looked at Bigon. 'I know I've seen it, but I just don't believe it!'

Adric and Nyssa were hearing the same news from Monarch himself. He leaned forward, staring at them with bulbous eyes, searching their faces for a response.

'So you're no more than androids?' asked Nyssa rather tactlessly when Monarch had finished speaking.

'No, girl! Don't irritate me, and above all don't disappoint me. I hold you to be intelligent. I have already explained, exactly and succintly, that we are fully integrated personalities with racial memories.'

'But not these?' She indicated the men who had brought them to Monarch.

'Ah no. There must be a class system, it is absolutely necessary for good government. They are second-class citizens. One could call them ... assisters.'

'Or slaves?'

'If you wish, girl. It is however, a very emotive word.'

'Very Flesh Time,' said Enlightenment scornfully.

'Flesh Time?'

'It is the name we give to the time of primitive, fleshly existence,' explained Enlightenment. 'In your human case, to the time of hunger and heart disease, arthritis, bronchitis, the common cold ...' She waved her hand, suggesting an unending list of human ailments.

Monarch leaned forward. 'Do you young people realise, I have overthrown the greatest tyranny in the universe—the tyranny of internal and external organs!'

'What about love?' asked Nyssa boldly.

'Love? What is love?'

'The exchange of two fantasies, your Majesty,' said Enlightenment.

'Thank you, Enlightenment.' Monarch stared at the two young people with burning eyes. 'Oh my children, I had hoped to convince you by my words, not hold you captive by the force of my assisters.'

All this time, Adric had been watching Monarch in utter fascination. 'You have convinced me, your Majesty.'

'My boy?'

'What you've achieved is almost beyond belief. You've performed miracles.'

Monarch beamed. 'Did you hear that, Enlightenment? We have been listening to voices from Earth for over fifty of their years. Did you ever hear a more intelligent statement? Release them, release them at once.' The guards stepped back, and Monarch beamed down at Adric. 'I can see you will be invaluable on my crusade!'

'Crusade?'

Monarch stared deep into Adric's eyes, and his deep throaty voice took on a hypnotic quality. 'To come to the aid of these unfortunate Earthlings. They are not as intelligent as you are. They war amongst themselves. They pay more attention to making weapons than producing food, yet two-thirds of them are starving. All these are problems of the Flesh Time. I come to rid them of it.'

'Perhaps they don't want to be rid of it?' suggested Nyssa.

'That's silly, Nyssa,' said Adric calmly. 'How could anyone want to live with all those troubles?'

Nyssa stared wonderingly at him.

'The boy is right!' said Monarch triumphantly.

'Think, girl,' urged Enlightenment. 'Think!'

Nyssa looked hard at her. 'Believe me, I am thinking.'

In the Doctor's quarters, Bigon was still doing his best to convince Tegan. 'What I say is true. We have been made immortal.'

'So it would seem,' agreed the Doctor. 'As long as you've got spare parts you can go on forever. All you really need is the raw materials.'

'That is the reason for Monarch's invasion of Earth. The previous visits established its suitability.'

'By George, that's it! Of course, that's it! He's after the silicon. Don't you see, Tegan? Silicon is one of the largest components of the Earth's crust. If he conquers Earth, he'll have all the silicon he wants, and the carbon too!'

Bigon went on with his appalling story, still in the same placid voice. 'He will begin by replacing the population of Earth with his own people.'

'How?' asked Tegan.

'Everything is planned. The landing will be peaceful. He has prepared a message of peace, offering the people of Earth the help of his superior alien intelligence. That is why he wants your help, to convince the people of Earth that he means them no harm.'

'But how is he going to dispose of three billion Earth people?'

'In the Mobilliary there is a poison. The Urbankans of the Flesh Time secreted it in a gland. It is the deadliest poison in the universe. It causes organic matter to collapse in upon itself.'

'What does that mean?'

'It means, girl, that one trillionth of a gramme would reduce you to the size of a grain of salt. With this

·poison, Monarch will depopulate the Earth.'

Monarch, assisted now by both Persuasion and Enlightenment, was painting his brave new world in glowing colours, for the benefit of Adric and the still-sceptical Nyssa. 'Surely you can see, my dear young people? We bring Enlightenment to the people of Earth.'

Nyssa glanced at the elegant figures on the thrones that flanked Monarch's own. 'Enlightenment—and Persuasion?'

'That too, of course.'

'Think of it, Nyssa,' urged Adric. 'A whole new technology, a whole new world. No more hunger, no more wars, fine schools—'

'Fine tyranny!'

Enlightenment said calmly, 'You must guard against the arrogance of the scientist, Nyssa. As a bioengineer, you more than most should marvel at the brilliance of our Monarch. He led us from the Urbankan slime to conquer first the land, then the elements, and finally to develop the greatest technology in the universe.'

'Do not be too hard on the child, Enlightenment,' said Monarch benignly. 'She has spirit and courage, a lively independence, qualities that will be of great use to us. She will come round to our way of seeing things in the end.'

'I won't come round to the acceptance of tyranny,' said Nyssa determinedly. 'I can never forget that my father was killed by a tyrant.'

'I think you're being a bit unfair,' protested Adric. 'You really can't compare his Majesty here to the Master.'

Monarch was greatly intrigued. 'And who is this Master?'

'A Time Lord, like the Doctor, your Majesty,' said Adric. 'He is the Doctor's greatest enemy.'

Bigon was revealing more horrors, still in the same placid voice. 'Unless Monarch is stopped, he will eventually destroy the Earth, just as he destroyed Urbanka.'

The Doctor looked surprised. 'I thought he said Urbanka's sun was a supernova?'

'That is a lie. Monarch exhausted Urbanka of its minerals, then polluted it with his technology. Eventually the pollution destroyed the ozone layer, and the ultra-violet light of the sun scorched Urbanka.' Bigon paused. 'All this was done in pursuit of his greatest plan—to travel faster than light. Monarch is obsessed with solving the riddle of the origin of the universe.'

'Got it!' said the Doctor suddenly. 'He thinks that to travel faster than light would be to go backwards in time, back to the Big Bang?'

'And beyond,' said Bigon solemnly. 'Monarch believes he will find himself there. He believes he is God.'

'I grieve for you, my child, that your father should have met such a fate.' There was honeyed sympathy in Monarch's voice. He turned to Adric. 'So this Doctor of yours is what is called a Time Lord?'

'Yes.'

'Whence comes his power?'

'From his people—the other Time Lords.'

'And who gave them their power?'

'I'm not sure. Sometimes the Doctor speaks of someone called Rassilon.'

'There is a legend about someone called Rassilon,' said Enlightenment suddenly. 'He is the one who is said to have found the Eye of Harmony.'

'You know very well, Enlightenment, that I regard such stories as mere superstition.'

'Yes, your Majesty.'

Monarch's bulging eyes glowed like fiery coals as he stared deep into Adric's. 'Tell me more of your Time Lord Doctor, boy. He seems a most agreeable person.'

'I suppose he is.'

'With a powerful mind?'

'Oh yes.'

'I like that. I like that very much. Tell me, has he any powers outside his machine?'

'Well, he's got two hearts,' said Adric helpfully.

'That must make him very vulnerable.'

'And he can put himself into a trance which suspends all life functions.'

'A useful gift. Now, tell me more of this machine of his.'

'The TARDIS?'

'What is the meaning of this name?'

'TARDIS—Time and Relative Dimensions In Space,' said Adric obligingly.

'Fascinating. The machine appears very small. Is it not uncomfortable for all of you?'

'Oh no. The inside is in a different dimension.'

'Indeed?'

Adric chattered on. 'It's large inside. In fact it's very large.'

'Why don't you shut up, Adric?' shouted Nyssa.

'Mind your manners, my dear,' said Monarch agreeably. But there was such menace in his voice that Nyssa fell silent. Once again, Monarch fixed Adric with his penetrating stare. 'Go on, my boy. What is inside this TARDIS?'

'Well, it's got a control room, a power room, a living quarter, a swimming bath. It's even got cloisters.'

'Cloisters?'

Enlightenment whispered to Monarch's ear. 'A cover-ed walkway, your Majesty, an architectural feature of educational and ecclesiastical establishments on Earth.'

'All these things are inside this TARDIS, boy?'

'Oh yes, your Majesty.'

'Fascinating!' Monarch fell to brooding, the great green head sunk on his chest. 'I would see these wonders for myself.'

'I'm sure the Doctor would be only too pleased to show you round,' offered Adric cheerfully. 'He's really the only one of us who understands how it operates.'

'Oh, I like that,' said Monarch enthusiastically. 'Would you ask the Doctor if he would let me see inside his TARDIS?'

'Of course, your Majesty. I'll go and see if he's in his quarters.'

Adric headed for the door. Nyssa made to follow, but Monarch growled, 'Not you. Take her!'

The warrior guard took hold of Nyssa's arm. He was inhumanly strong and there was nothing she could do.

Monarch smiled down at her. 'I have other plans for you, my child.'

Nyssa struggled wildly, but it was quite useless.

'What are you going to do?'

Monarch said, 'Do not be afraid. One only harms that which one fears. Why should I harm you—when soon you will be one of us?'

8

Tegan's Gamble

'He must be stopped at all costs, Doctor,' said Bigon.

The Doctor paced about the room, thinking hard. 'I quite agree. But if you feel like this, why haven't you acted before?'

'I can feel and I can speak, but I cannot act. I am powerless alone. I have free will, but built into my circuits is a fail-safe mechanism. Any aggressive action is immediately signalled and baulked.'

'Then the only course of action I can think of is to go along with Monarch, appear to co-operate.'

'There may not be much time for that,' warned Bigon. 'Sooner or later he is bound to make you as I am. All of you.'

Tegan gave him a horrified look. 'You mean he'll kill us?'

'It is not death. First you are hypnotised—the Urbankans all have great hypnotic powers. Under hypnosis you are made to recall your whole life. This is recorded on a micro-chip. Your body is disposed of, and you are remade, as I was.

Tegan put her hand to her mouth in horror. 'No! No! No!'

The Doctor patted her shoulder. 'It's all right, Tegan, it's all right. Leave everything to me.'

'I'm sick and tired of leaving everything to you!'

Giving her a couple more awkward pats, the Doctor turned back to Bigon. 'Can you show me the ship? Controls, population, everything. I'll need all the information you can give me.'

'Very well, Doctor, I will do as you ask. But we must hurry. Soon Monarch will become suspicious of my absence.'

The Doctor picked up his space-pack. 'Let's go, then.'

Tegan looked at him in astonishment. 'You're not planning to go wandering off on a tour?'

'Do try to keep calm, Tegan.'

'Calm! Look, all we've got to do is get out of here. We've just got to get back to the TARDIS and get away.'

'If you'll just stop thinking about yourself for once.'

'I'm not thinking about myself! We've got to get back to Earth and warn them.'

'Warn them of what? Who'll believe us? We'd just be laughed at.'

'The least we can do is try.'

'We will try—another way.'

Bigon had moved to the door. 'Doctor, we must go now.'

'Yes, I'm coming.' The Doctor turned back to Tegan. 'You wait here. You'll be safe enough, and I won't be long.'

'I won't stay here by myself,' said Tegan determinedly.

'Oh yes you will.' The Doctor nodded to the sabotaged monopticon. 'In here you can't be seen or heard. Out there you can. Bigon, you go a little in front of me. That will lure the monopticon out there away from me, and I can surprise it.'

'Very well,' Bigon moved through the door.

Tegan said frantically, 'Doctor, please don't leave me alone here.'

'Sssh,' said the Doctor, and disappeared.

Bigon was moving slowly along the corridor, the monopticon bobbing along behind him.

The Doctor crept up behind the globe and gave it a quick burst from his sonic screwdriver. Immediately the monopticon began spinning helplessly.

Bigon studied it for a moment. 'I see. You reversed the magnetic field.'

'That's right. That's how we'll deal with all of them. Come on!'

They hurried off down the corridor.

Bigon indicated the Doctor's space-pack. 'You had better put that on, Doctor. There are many parts of the ship where you will need it.'

Nyssa was standing helplessly before Enlightenment, who had come down from her throne and was leaning over her. Enlightenment's eyes seemed to blaze with an unearthly light, and her gentle voice was utterly compelling. 'Your eyes are getting heavier. They are getting heavier ... and heavier ... and heavier ... Nyssa's head began to nod, and her eyes closed. 'Now you are asleep. Soon you will recall all your past life for us, and then you will be relieved of the Flesh Time.'

Enlightenment beckoned to the warrior gaurds. 'Take her to the Mobilliary.'

As the warriors led Nyssa away, Monarch said, 'Well done, Enlightenment.'

'Her mind is very strong, your Majesty. I cannot change her thinking, as you have done with the boy, but once she is free of the Flesh Time, we shall be able to control her.'

Persuasion was staring at one of the monitors, which was showing nothing but a kind of whirling blur. 'The monopticon on linkway seven appears to have developed a fault.'

Enlightenment studied the display. 'The magnetic field must have reversed.'

'And it was the Doctor who reversed it,' roared Monarch. 'He will be dealt with! They will all be dealt with! My patience is not inexhaustible!'

In the computer library, all was calm as usual, the robed scholars working tirelessly at their consoles, a watchful monopticon hovering overhead. A shiny red cricket ball rolled across the floor. The monopticon glided after the strange object, while the Doctor slipped into the library and swiftly disabled the monopticon, setting it spinning wildly.

Retrieving his cricket ball, the Doctor turned to the doorway and waved, and Bigon followed him into the room.

Angrily Monarch studied yet another useless monitor screen. 'It would appear that the Doctor has reached the library. Much good may it do him.' A thought struck Monarch. 'Unless perhaps Bigon is with him!'

Persuasion said, 'I have not seen Bigon for some considerable time, your Majesty.'

Another monitor screen showed Adric wandering along a corridor.

'The boy appears to be lost,' said Enlightenment.

'He is an intelligent lad,' said Monarch loftily. 'He will find his way.'

Bigon operated a wall control-panel and said, 'You may remove your helmet to conserve your air supply, Doctor. The life-support system is now working.' He indicated a red light glowing at the top of the panel.

Taking off the space-pack, the Doctor went over to the scholars, who worked steadily at their consoles, completely ignoring him.

'The ship's course is maintained from here?'

'Yes. Most of the time, the control is automatic.'

'Then what are this lot doing?'

'They are doing what they have been doing for many centuries, trying to find formulae to move the ship faster than light—and not without some indications of success.' Bigon smiled ironically. 'Monarch hopes that in a mere thousand years or so, he will be going backwards in time, for a rendezvous with himself—the Creator!'

In the Mobilliary, the mandarin Lin Futu stood waiting, surrounded by his robed assisters. As the warrior guards brought Nyssa to him he said, 'Leave her.'

The warriors moved away, and Lin Futu beckoned

two of the assisters. They led Nyssa to a kind of upright cabinet—like a coffin—connected to a maze of equipment. Nyssa stood unresisting inside the cabinet, while electrodes were fastened to her forehead. The metal door of the cabinet was closed, and there was a low hum of power.

Lin Futu worked impassively at the controls monitoring the recorded flow of memories from Nyssa's mind.

After what seemed like hours of wandering, Adric found his way to the Doctor's quarters—which were empty except for a distraught Tegan.

'Well, where is he then?'

'How should I know? He's gone wandering off again. Adric, we've got to get off this ship. We must or we'll all be dead—or worse than dead!'

'Rubbish! Monarch has no reason to harm us. He wants our help! Adric's eyes were positively shining with enthusiasm. 'The Doctor was quite right about these Urbankans. They're light-years ahead of us in technology.'

'Silicon chips!' Tegan hissed the words as if they were swear-words.

'You know then?'

'I know a lot more than you. Now get out of my way.' Tegan headed for the door.

Adric barred her way. 'Where are you going?'

'To the TARDIS!'

'Why?'

'To try to get off this ship. Someone has to!'

'You're being very silly, Tegan. Anyway, you can't even work the TARDIS.'

'I'm going to have a heck of a good try!'

'But why? What's all the panic? I can't think what you're in such a state about. The Urbankans are benefactors.'

'Ha!' said Tegan, with terrible scorn.

'Monarch is absolutely charming. He asked me very politely if he could see over the TARDIS. I was just coming to ask the Doctor.'

Tegan was rapidly losing patience. 'Listen, Adric, you can either come with me, or get out of my way. Now, which is it to be?'

Adric looked worriedly at her, wondering why she just couldn't seem to understand. After his long talk with Monarch, everything was perfectly clear to him. 'Tegan, everything's all right, I tell you. In any case, you can't even get into the TARDIS.'

'Oh can't I?' Tegan fished in her pocket and held out the TARDIS key. 'The Doctor gave me this when we first left. Forgotten that, hadn't you?'

'Oh good,' said Adric brightly, and held out his hand. 'I'll take that.'

Fiercely Tegan snatched her hand away. 'You will not!' I'm warning you, Adric, get out of my way!'

Adric saw that it was his duty to save Tegan from herself. 'No. I refuse to let you do anything so silly.'

Tegan tried to push past him, Adric grappled with her—then Tegan gave him a shove that held all the strength of desperation. Adric staggered back; his ankle turned under him and he fell heavily, striking his head against the bunk.

Unaware of what had happened, Tegan fled frantically down the corridor.

Lin Futu studied the dials in front of him. 'She will soon be ready. About two more minutes ...'

Bigon strode into the Flora Chamber, the indoor jungle that Adric and Nyssa had found earlier. The Aborigine assisters went on with tending the plants, totally ignoring him as usual. The Flora Chamber monopticon bobbed inquisitively after Bigon—and the Doctor slipped up behind with his sonic screwdriver and set it spinning dizzily.

As yet another monitor blurred, Persuasion said urgently. 'The Doctor is in the Flora Chamber with Bigon. I caught a glimpse of them before the monitor failed.'

'First the library, and now the Flora Chamber,' mused Monarch. 'It would seem that friend Bigon is giving the Doctor a guided tour.'

'Is it wise to permit this, your Majesty?'

For all the deference in his tone, Persuasion's question did not please Monarch.

'So—now my other Minister doubts my wisdom?'

'I beg your Majesty's pardon.'

'I should think so,' said Monarch huffily. 'I should think so indeed!'

The Doctor and Bigon were standing by the edge of the little pool. The Doctor studied the riot of tropical vegetation around him, and squinted at the blazing light. 'Intensified ultra-violet for increased photo-synthesis?'

Bigon nodded. 'Yes. This is all that was saved of Urbanka.'

The Doctor rubbed his chin. 'I wonder why. It's a source of oxygen, I suppose.'

'For those who need it.'

'Point taken!'

'This place is also the graveyard of the others taken from Earth.'

'There were others, then?'

'Many. After the initial experiments only those of the highest intelligence were allowed to live on—as I was.'

The Doctor stared down into the pool. A frog stared balefully back at him. 'And the frogs?'

'They are—hosts. They ensure a supply of the poison with which Monarch will depopulate Earth.'

For once Tegan's sense of direction didn't play her false. Before very long she found her way back to the huge deserted control area and the familiar blue shape of the TARDIS. Tegan hurried over to it, opened the door and went inside.

Once in the control room she studied the many sided central control console. She had seen the Doctor work it often enough. Adric and Nyssa, she knew, could operate it too, after a fashion, though usually under the Doctor's supervision. But coming as she did from a less technologically advanced civilisation, Tegan was at a disadvantage. Moreover, she had made little attempt to understand the working of the TARDIS, since her only interest was in persuading the Doctor to use it to get her home. But Tegan was no fool. She had seen the Doctor take off in the TARDIS often enough, and her training as an air-hostess had given her some basic technical knowledge.

With a sudden surge of hope, she remembered that Adric had already programmed the TARDIS to take them to Earth when Monarch's ship had somehow diverted them.

Presumably those settings were still locked in. If she could simply get the TARDIS to take off, there was at least a chance that the journey to Earth, perhaps even the landing as well, would take place automatically.

Tegan stared hard at the console, drew a deep breath—and set to work.

9

Death Warrant

Monarch sighed, as yet another monitor cut out. 'The guided tour continues, it seems.'

Enlightenment said, 'They are now in the Mobilliary, your Majesty.'

'The girl Nyssa is there at this time also,' Persuasion reminded him. 'She is in the first stage of preparation. The process is being supervised by Lin Futu.'

Monarch sat brooding on his throne, and said nothing. He was beginning to wonder if it had been wise to permit the Doctor and his companions so much freedom. Unfortunately, such was Monarch's immense conceit that he found it almost impossible to admit his mistake. And a mistake that is not acknowledged cannot be corrected.

Distracted from his work, Lin Futu stared curiously at the monopticon which seemed to be spinning in a most peculiar fashion. He looked reprovingly at the Doctor. 'What have you done to this monopticon?'

It was Bigon who replied, forcing himself, with an effort, to lie in a good cause. 'The Doctor was merely trying a small experiment. No permanent harm has been done. Monarch has commanded me to show the Doctor the ship. I hope we do not intrude?'

'Not at all,' said Lin Futu courteously. 'But perhaps you will permit me to continue with my work?'

Bigon bowed, and Lin Futu turned back to his controls. 'This is where the metamorphoses are performed,' said Bigon. 'Lin Futu is usually in charge. This way, Doctor.' He led the Doctor to a wall which consisted entirely of little drawers, thousands of them, row upon row of them, from floor to ceiling. 'Here in these drawers are stored the Urbankans, the future inhabitants of Earth.'

'What an appalling thought.'

Curious, and a little suspicious, Lin Futu edged closer to them.

He heard Bigon say, 'If Monarch's plan is to be foiled, Doctor, all these must be destroyed. He has infected every Urbanken with his own insane ambitions.'

The Doctor nodded, looking at the endless rows of drawers. 'Quite a tall order!'

Lin Futu had heard enough. He moved back to his control console, hesitated for a moment, then switched it off and glided silently from the Mobilliary.

Bigon opened a tiny drawer and closed it again. 'This drawer was once my prison for a hundred years, Doctor. Punishment for my one and only act of revolt.' He led the Doctor to another wall where a crystal flask was clipped to the centre of a bulkhead, almost like a trophy or award set up on display. 'And this is the poison!'

The Doctor looked at the flask for a moment. It

seemed almost unbelievable that so small a container could hold death for an entire planet. But he had seen too much of Urbankan technology to doubt Bigon's word.

He followed Bigon to the area just vacated by lin Futu. They stood looking at the blank-faced steel coffin.

Bigon said, 'This is how the process works, Doctor. The subject is hypnotised, the memory recorded. Once that is done the subject is terminated and the body can be used to fertilise the Flora Chamber.' Bigon broke off, studying the dials. 'By Zeus, there is someone already in there!'

'Who?'

'One of you—it must be!'

Bigon wrenched open the front of the cabinet, and to his horror the Doctor saw the still form of Nyssa.

'Quickly, Bigon!'

Bigon helped the Doctor to lift the unconscious girl from the cabinet, ignored by Lin Futu's robed assisters.

They laid her on a nearby couch, and the Doctor leant over her, snapping his fingers in front of her face. 'Nyssa! Wake up! Wake up!'

Nyssa opened her eyes. 'Oh Doctor! Thank goodness it's you!' She struggled to a half-sitting position and hugged him.

Gently the Doctor helped her to sit up properly. 'Are you all right?'

'I will be, in a minute. They were going to kill me, Doctor, turn me into a robot ...'

'Yes, I'm afraid they were, the devils. Where's Adric?'

'He's all right, I think. They sent him to look for you.'

She struggled to remember. 'They want to get into the TARDIS.'

'Oh do they!' said the Doctor indignantly. 'We'll see about that!'

Adric groaned and sat up, rubbing his aching head. But he was young and strong, and it hadn't been that heavy a blow. Painfully, he struggled to his feet, and staggering a little, he stumbled out of the room.

Lin Futu said, 'I overheard them quite clearly, your Majesty. They were plotting the destruction of the Urbankan people.'

'You have done well, Lin Futu, very well indeed. Fear not, I shall deal with them. Bigon will be decircuited, and the Doctor destroyed. See to it, Persuasion.'

'At once, your Majesty!' Persuasion bowed and hurried away.

Monarch settled back on his throne. 'So perish all who threaten my mission!'

Nyssa was fully recovered by now. The Doctor and Bigon were conferring in low voices.

'Now listen, Bigon,' said the Doctor urgently. 'Can we expect any support from those who are as you? Kurkutji, Lin Futu, the others with intelligence and some free will.'

'No, Doctor. As you say, they have, like me, at least some measure of free will. But they have been corrupted by power. They have been promised as I was, domination over their respective ethnic groups—or at least over those of them whom Monarch allows to survive. I have not dared to speak, lest they betray me to Monarch.'

'He does intend to leave some Earth people alive then?' asked Nyssa.

'So he claims. I believe he lies. He will empty Earth of all life, and replace its population with Urbankans. But the others believe him. They believe they will be rulers.'

'I suppose it was a difficult offer to refuse.'

'Not for me,' said Bigon firmly. 'In a civilised world there is no substitute for democracy.'

The Doctor was thinking hard. 'Is there nowhere on this ship where we can hide and prepare a plan?'

'Nowhere.'

'What about weapons?'

'There is an armoury—but it is in the throne room.'

'Then our only hope is to get back to the TARDIS and warn Earth. It looks as if Tegan was right after all—' Suddenly a thought struck the Doctor and he pointed to one of the robed assisters. 'What about these things? Are they any use to us?'

Bigon followed the Doctor's thought. 'Not as they are. But perhaps if there was some way of altering their circuits ...'

Nyssa jumped up. 'Doctor, lend me your sonic screwdriver!'

'What for?'

'I want to try something.'

Puzzled, the Doctor handed her the screwdriver. Nyssa studied it. 'Presumably there's a built-in electric charge?' The Doctor nodded. Nyssa held out her hand. 'Your propelling pencil too, please.' The Doctor passed it over, and Nyssa wound the top of the pencil to expose a little of the lead.

Suddenly Adric burst into the room. 'Thank goodness I've found you, Doctor!'

The Doctor looked at him in concern. Adric was wide-eyed and dishevelled, and there was a purple bruise on his forehead.

'What's happened to you, Adric? What's the matter?'

'It's Tegan. She's gone to the TARDIS.'

'Best place for her, I should think.'

'You don't understand! She's going to try and fly it. She wants to take it to Earth.'

'Oh good grief!' said the Doctor, and sat down on the bunk.

He immediately jumped up again as Persuasion and Lin Futu marched into the room, flanked by two warrior guards.

'Take them,' said Persuasion coldly. The mandarin-robed assisters left their tasks and closed in on the Doctor and his companions.

Persuasion glanced angrily up at the spinning monopticon. Reaching up, he made a quick adjustment which restored it to normal. It bobbed across the room after Persuasion as he strode towards the captive group. He looked at the Doctor, Adric and Nyssa. 'Where is the fourth—the girl.'

'She's gone back to my TARDIS,' said the Doctor. 'You can't reach her in there.'

'Can she fly this machine of yours?'

'No,' said the Doctor definitely. 'Only I can do that.' He had a feeling that his knowledge of TARDIS technology might be his only bargaining point.

Adric said, 'Well, Tegan's going to try, Doctor.'

Persuasion looked sharply at him. 'This girl can operate the TARDIS?'

'No,' said the Doctor definitely. 'She'd be very foolish even to try—and she certainly won't succeed if she does.'

In the throne room, Monarch was following the scene in the Mobilliary on his now restored monitor. Most of the other monitor screens were also working again—Persuasion had despatched assisters to remedy the Doctor's sabotage—and on one of them Monarch could see the TARDIS.

Monarch spoke his thoughts aloud while Enlightenment listened intently. 'So, the girl is in the TARDIS. But the Doctor says that she cannot work it. He says that only he can work it—if this is so, then I must spare him.'

Persuasion's voice came from the Mobilliary. 'Shall I proceed to destroy your Majesty's enemies?'

Monarch shouted. 'No! Wait, Persuasion. I would consider further.'

Tegan was still working frantically at the TARDIS console. She had seen the take-off sequence many times, but somehow she just couldn't reproduce it correctly.

Sometimes nothing happened, sometimes the console groaned and throbbed, rather like a car being driven with the brake on. Once the time rotor had actually begun its familiar movement up and down . . . but almost immediately it had slowed to a halt.

Tegan was becoming frantic. She made a desperate effort to calm her mind. She stood quietly for a moment and tried to imagine that she was the Doctor, about to carry out a routine take-off. She began the take-off sequence for what seemed the hundredth time: you did this, and this and this . . . Tegan found that her hands were moving as if of their own accord.

Lights flashed, needles flickered and the time rotor began moving steadily up and down. She'd done it. The TARDIS was in flight.

Tegan stood back, wringing her hands in unbelieving delight. She had, of course, no way of knowing that she had just signed the Doctor's death warrant.

The scanner system in the throne room picked up a strange wheezing, groaning sound, and Enlightenment said, 'Your Majesty, look!' She pointed to one of the monitors.

Monarch looked and was just in time to see the TARDIS fade slowly away. The corrugated green skin of Monarch's face was twisted with rage. 'So! The Doctor lied. The TARDIS goes! Indeed, it has gone! Any fool can operate it. So much for the Doctor's technology. Without his craft, he is useless to me. So be it! Destroy him, Persuasion. Do you hear me? Destroy him!'

There had been a kind of frozen tableau in the Mobilliary as everyone waited for Monarch to make up his mind. Bigon had been put upon the operating table where he lay calmly waiting.

Suddenly the waxwork-like scene came to violent

life. Persuasion pointed to Bigon. 'Decircuit that!' He whirled round on the Doctor. 'Kill him!' One of the warriors raised his sword, but despite all Monarch's persuasive powers Adric's loyalty to the Doctor was deep-seated and strong. 'No,' he shouted and hurled himself upon the guard.

With his free hand, the guard caught Adric's wrists and held him captive. Adric struggled wildly, but he was helpless against the machine strength of the warrior's android body.

At a nod from Persuasion, one of the robed assisters caught the Doctor's arms and forced him to his knees. The second guard drew his sword. Stepping up to the Doctor, he raised his sword for the killing blow.

10

Reprieved

It was Nyssa who saved the Doctor. She had been standing unnoticed in the background, ignored because nobody considered her a threat. Suddenly she darted forward, sonic screwdriver in one hand, propelling pencil in the other. In the second before the blow fell, she applied screwdriver and pencil to the warrior's wristband. Immediately the warrior froze, sword raised high, like some ancient statue. While everyone else was still staring in astonishment, Nyssa ran to the warrior holding Adric and immobilised him as well.

Persuasion stepped back, drawing a compact raygun from his pocket and trained it on the Doctor.

'No!' shouted Adric again and threw himself in front of the Doctor.

For just a moment, Persuasion hesitated.

In the throne room Monarch snapped, 'Persuasion! Do not harm the boy. Wait!'

Persuasion stepped back, his gun still trained on Adric, awaiting further instructions.

Monarch's mood had changed and he now seemed almost amused by the drama being played out before him. 'The boy has great courage, Enlightenment.'

'And the girl an almost Urbankan intelligence. The graphite of the pencil conducted the power of the sonic device, causing a short circuit.'

'Precisely, Enlightenment. What admirable invention.'

In the Mobilliary, Adric raised his voice. 'I don't know if you can hear me, your Majesty?'

Monarch leaned forward, intrigued. 'I hear you, boy.'

Gazing up at the monopticon, Adric said. 'With the greatest respect, your Majesty, I cannot join you if any harm is done to the Doctor.'

Monarch was delighted. 'Oh, splendid boy. What courage! What loyalty. What a help he will be once those qualities are transferred to *me*!' He raised his voice. 'Persuasion, stay the execution and bring them all to me.' He chuckled. 'Perhaps you had better confiscate the Doctor's sonic device!'

Persuasion swung round and covered Nyssa with his ray-gun. 'The sonic device, please.'

Reluctantly, Nyssa handed it over.

Persuasion smiled. 'You may keep the pencil.' He turned. 'Release the Doctor!'

The robed androids let go of the Doctor and stepped back. The Doctor got to his feet. Now the gun was trained on him.

'You will turn out your pockets, Doctor.'

'Yes, I think I will,' said the Doctor, as if he'd just thought of it himself. Fishing in his pockets he produced his diary, an optician's eyepiece, a cricket ball and a piece of string.

One by one Persuasion took the articles, studied them and put them to one side—with the exception of the diary which he handed back to the Doctor. He held up the eyepiece. 'What is this?'

'Eyeglass,' said the Doctor. He pointed to his right eye. 'Bit short-sighted in this one.'

Persuasion handed it back and held up the piece of string. 'And this?'

'It's just a piece of string.'

The string was handed over. Next it was the turn of the cricket ball. 'This?'

'Cricket ball. It's a memento. I used to bowl a very good googly, you know. Took six wickets for New South Wales with that ball.'

Persuasion shrugged and handed back the cricket ball. 'His Majesty wishes to see you, now! All of you.' He turned to Lin Futu, who was in the process of removing two circuits from Bigon's chest cavity. 'See that the motor circuits of these assisters are replaced.' He gestured with his gun at the Doctor and his companions. 'You will precede me, please.'

As Persuasion herded the Doctor and the others from the room, Bigon swung his legs down from the table, and walked away. His face was expressionless and he moved with the impassive deliberation of the androids—naturally enough, since he was no longer Bigon. All that was essentially Bigon was contained in the two micro-chips in Lin Futu's hand.

In the TARDIS control room, Tegan saw with unbelieving horror that the time rotor was slowing down.
It moved slower, slower, and then stopped.

Tegan stared anxiously at it. The journey had scarce-
ly started. Surely she couldn't have reached Earth
already. She hurried to the scanner controls. After a
couple of false starts she managed to get the scanner
working.

As usual, it showed what was immediately outside
the TARDIS—and what was outside the TARDIS at
the moment was not Heathrow airport but the massive
hull of Monarch's ship. Tegan had failed to apply the
necessary power boost at the moment of take-off, and
the TARDIS had materialised in space not far from the
spaceship's hull. Now it was trapped in the spaceship's
forcefield. Side by side, spaceship and TARDIS were
sailing towards Earth together.

Tegan rushed to the console and then drew back. 'Oh
no you don't, my girl. Best thing you can do is leave
well alone.'

Persuasion was marching the Doctor and party along
one of the linkways on the outer hull of the ship. The
Doctor glanced out of the windows and stopped,
astonished to see the TARDIS floating in space just
opposite him.

Persuasion glanced out of the window and smiled. 'It
seems that your craft, Doctor, like the poor, is always
with us. I would prefer not to keep his Majesty waiting.'
He waved them onwards.

When they entered the throne room, one of Monarch's

monitors was showing the TARDIS floating in space.

Monarch pointed to it and chuckled. 'It would seem, Doctor, that your machine is reluctant to break free from mine.'

'Can't imagine why,' said the Doctor rather impolitely.

'A more considerate guest perhaps than its owner?'

'Is it usual for a host to kill a guest?'

'In certain rarefied circles. Your life was forfeit, Doctor, because you were plotting against me.'

Once in Monarch's presence, Adric seemed once more to be under his domination. He gave the Doctor a reproachful look. 'Is that true, Doctor?'

Like Bigon, the Doctor was prepared to lie in a good cause—such as his own survival. 'Not at all. My actions were motivated purely by scientific curiosity.'

'Not as they were reported to me.'

'Reports can be garbled, your Majesty.'

'This one wasn't. Was it scientific curiosity which caused you to interfere with my monopticons?'

'Me? I wouldn't dream of interfering with your monopticons.'

Monarch waved an expansive claw. 'Enough of these foolish recriminations. I propose to demonstrate my moral superiority by sparing your life, Doctor. I am not, as you would have others believe a wanton destroyer. However, I must protect myself and my mission. The girl Nyssa will be held hostage. Provided your behaviour is restrained, she will not be harmed. Take care that you do not become the cause of her destruction.' Monarch waved a paw at Persuasion. 'Take the girl back to Lin Futu. Let him sedate her, and await my orders as to her disposition.'

Persuasion herded Nyssa away at gunpoint, and Monarch looked benignly around the throne room. 'Control! Let there be a recreational! Let my eyes be restored from the strain of looking at monitor screens affected by the Doctor's scientific curiosity! I would have my family together under my benevolent gaze.' Monarch pointed a stubby green finger at the Doctor. 'You have my permission to withdraw.'

'Thank you, your Majesty.' Making the best of a bad job, the Doctor bowed politely and left the throne room.

Adric glanced up at Monarch, who waved him graciously away. Adric bowed and followed the Doctor.

Monarch settled back on his throne, preening himself. 'You must admit, Enlightenment, that that was brilliantly handled.'

'Brilliantly, your Majesty.'

'The boy Adric cannot fail to be with me now.'

Persuasion re-entered the control room. 'The girl Nyssa is secured and sedated your Majesty.'

'Good. And the Doctor and the boy?'

'They should be at the recreational, your Majesty.'

Monarch glanced at the appropriate monitor screen. In the recreation hall the Aborigines were giving yet another rendition of one of their interminable war dances. Monarch touched a control and the monopticon provided a panoramic view of the room. It held for a moment on Bigon, standing impassively on the lower level, his face quite blank.

'I am glad that Bigon has been decircuited,' said Persuasion 'With respect, it should have been done

102

centuries ago.'

Monarch frowned, displeased as always when his judgment was questioned.

Hurriedly Persuasion said, 'I will check up on the Doctor and the boy, your Majesty.' He hurried from the throne room.

As Adric and the Doctor re-entered their quarters the Doctor was saying loudly, 'I'm sorry about the way I've behaved Adric, I really am.'

'That's all right, Doctor,' said Adric generously. 'There's no real harm done. Nothing will happen to Nyssa as long as you don't do anything else silly. You have been behaving rather badly, you know, Doctor.'

'I know, that's what I'm so sorry about. I think I've been entirely mistaken about Monarch.'

'I'm so glad to hear you say that.'

The Doctor looked narrowly at him, wondering how Monarch had managed this instant conversion. It wasn't hypnotism, thought the Doctor, nothing so simple as that. It was a kind of direct, personal domination, as though Monarch had been able to reach inside Adric's mind and actually change his way of thinking. There seemed to be some extraordinary link between them. It was clear too that Monarch had some quite genuine concern for the boy—a fact which had already saved the Doctor's life.

Whatever the influence was, it was going to be a difficult and delicate business to counter it. And for the moment, the best thing to do was to play along.

The Doctor glanced up at the now repaired

monopticon, and raised his voice again. 'He's an autocrat, of course, but essentially a benevolent one.'

'Oh yes, he is,' said Adric earnestly.

Monarch was listening in enraptured silence. It was, after all, his favourite subject.

The Doctor's voice echoed clearly through the throne room. 'Oh, he's ruthless, of course, anyone can see that. But great leaders have to be ruthless. It's his sense of mission, his sheer breadth of vision, that's so breathtaking.'

Then Adric's voice. 'Yes it is, isn't it?'

'He could easily have had me killed,' the Doctor's voice went on. 'Why didn't he? It must be because he's essentially benevolent.'

'Exactly what I've been trying to tell you all along, Doctor.'

'I know, Adric, and I'm sorry I refused to listen. At the very earliest opportunity I shall request permission to see Monarch. I shall seek an audience, and make my peace with him.'

Adric was taking in all this rubbish with keen attention.

The Doctor drew a deep breath. The one thing about flattering tyrants, he thought, was that it was almost impossible to overdo it. 'I'm not given to exaggeration, Adric, but, do you know, a kind of blinding revelation has come to me—like a vision. Monarch is the greatest being in the universe as we know it.'

Monarch was leaning back on his throne, positively quaking in an ecstasy of self-adulation. How wonderful he must be when even his enemies praised him.

The Doctor felt that if he had to say one more word in praise of Monarch it would choke him. 'Hadn't we better be getting to the recreational, Adric? I got the impression Monarch wanted us to be there?'

'All right,' said Adric obligingly, and they set off for the recreation hall.

As they came into the hall, the Doctor saw with some relief that the Aborigine war dance was just finishing. It was succeeded almost immediately by the Mayan folk-dance, which was no great improvement. The Doctor saw Bigon amongst the audience, staring blankly ahead of him. His eyes caught the Doctor's for a moment, but showed no sign of life or recognition. The sight of Bigon and the thought of what had been done to him strengthened the Doctor's anger.

Glancing round, he saw Persuasion come into the hall from the other side. He was looking keenly about him, and when he saw the Doctor and Adric he seemed to relax.

'Been told to keep an eye on us,' thought the Doctor. 'We must make sure he doesn't see anything to upset him.'

The Doctor led Adric to an isolated seat at the end of the gallery, and they sat down. The Doctor leaned back, smiling and relaxed as he watched the show. When he spoke however, his voice was low and urgent. 'Keep watching the show, Adric, but listen to what I'm saying, and listen hard.'

'What's the matter, Doctor?'

'You are, you young idiot,' said the Doctor fiercely. 'You're not so much stupid as idealistic. It must come from your deprived delinquent background. Monarch isn't the greatest being in the known universe, but he well may be the greatest force for evil. He'll destroy Earth and probably a whole lot of other planets as well, unless he's stopped. So we've got to stop him, while there's still time!'

Adric was horrified. 'But back there you were saying—'

'Back there he could hear us. Here, he can't. I was just playing for time.'

'You're wrong, you know, Doctor,' said Adric obstinately. 'Monarch is civilised—'

'Do you want to save Nyssa?'

'Yes, of course I do.'

'Then shut up and listen!' The Doctor started talking as though his life depended on it—which in fact it did.

11

Riot!

The Doctor knew he was taking a terrible risk trying to win Adric over. The influence of Monarch was tremendously strong. Perhaps it would prove so strong that Adric would go immediately to Monarch and betray him. If that happened Monarch would have no further reason to keep the Doctor and Nyssa alive. Adric, his loyal convert, would be enough.

Monarch had to be fought with his own weapons. The Doctor knew he had to reach Adric not only through his reason, but by displacing the influence of Monarch's personality with his own.

The Doctor talked long and earnestly, recalling all that had happened since they had arrived on Monarch's ship. 'Monarch isn't concerned with bringing civilisation, Adric, he has the greatest contempt for anyone but himself. He wants to rob Earth of its mineral wealth in order to travel faster than light. And if that doesn't convince you, why does he carry deadly poison on the ship?'

'*Poison?*' For the first time Adric seemed to waver.

The Doctor told him what he had learned from Bigon of the Urbankan poison, its effects, and its final deadly purpose. 'The poison is stored in the Mobilliary. If his mission really is peaceful, *why does he carry a poison that can wipe out everyone on Earth?*'

'Research?' suggested Adric feebly.

'Do you really believe that?'

'Then why did Monarch spare your life? He could easily have killed you.'

'He doesn't want to upset you,' said the Doctor grimly. 'Not yet. He wants to make use of you, in the first stages of his mission to Earth. His subjects are all synthetic. Even the superior ones like Enlightenment and Persuasion have something mechanical about them. However sophisticated their circuitry, they are still basically machines—and so are his captives from Earth. Monarch needs you, because you still have emotions, you're flesh and blood. If you speak up for him on Earth you can allay their suspicions, delay opposition, until it's too late.' The Doctor drew a deep breath. 'I've been telling you the truth, Adric. Now, are you with me?'

'I think so ...'

'Make up your mind. There isn't much time.'

'What are you going to do?'

The Doctor said grimly, 'I haven't the slightest intention of telling you—not until I know you're with me.' He paused. 'Well?'

Perhaps the threat of exclusion from the Doctor's confidence did the trick, but Adric managed to produce one of his familiar cheeky grins. 'Yes, all right, *yes*! I'm with you!'

The Doctor returned the smile. 'Good. We'd better get moving then. Keep it casual!' The Doctor rose slowly, yawned and stretched, and strolled from the gallery.

Trying to look equally relaxed, Adric followed.

On the throne room monitor Monarch watched them leave. 'The Doctor is tired, Enlightenment. So is the boy.'

'It is a prime disadvantage of the Flesh Time, your Majesty.'

'Soon we shall relieve them of that burden.'

As the Doctor and Adric moved along the linkways towards the Mobilliary they passed a still-spinning monopticon.

The Doctor grinned. 'We're in luck, they haven't put that one right yet.'

'What are you going to do?'

'Get some allies if I can. There's the Mobilliary. Nyssa's through there somewhere.' The Doctor fished out his eyepiece. 'I can use this to distract the monopticon without actually disabling it. It won't scan us, but with any luck it won't draw attention to us either. Be ready to take over from me as soon as we're inside.'

They slipped into the Mobilliary and the Doctor looked round cautiously. Nyssa lay on one of the smaller operating tables, apparently in a drugged sleep. Lin Futu was working near by and the mandarin-robed assisters were quietly busy as usual.

With Adric close behind him, the Doctor crept up to the hovering monopticon and suddenly held his eyepiece in line with its lens. The monopticon froze in place as if hypnotised. The Doctor nodded to Adric, who took the eyepiece from his hand, trying to keep it in position.

'It's important to hold it steady,' whispered the Doctor. 'It has a cobalt ring with a high-flux density.'

'Right,' whispered Adric. The Doctor tiptoed away.

Apparently unseen, he made his way over to the wall of storage drawers and reached for the one that Bigon had called his prison. Hoping he'd remembered the right drawer, the Doctor pulled it open. Sure enough, there inside were the two extra micro-chips that made Bigon a personality rather than an unthinking android.

The Doctor turned to look for Lin Futu, and jumped when he found that the mandarin had come silently up behind him.

'What are you doing?' demanded Lin Futu sternly.

'Saving your life, I hope!'

Lin Futu turned to summon his assisters, but the Doctor said rapidly, 'Please, here me out. You are in great danger. You, and all your people on Earth!'

Intrigued, in spite of himself, Lin Futu hesitated . . .

Monarch and Enlightenment were still watching the recreational on the monitors.

Persuasion entered and bowed. 'All seems in order, your Majesty. The Doctor and the boy watched the recreational for a while, became tired and then left.'

Monarch nodded carelessly. 'I know, I saw our friends retire.' He glanced across the row of monitors and found one which showed only a patch of blank wall. 'Mobilliary, why have you not changed your scan? Control, report on that monitor!'

The computer said, 'Cobalt high-flux density present.'

Monarch sighed. 'Don't tell me the Doctor's on the prowl again. What a pest! Persuasion!'

Once again, Persuasion hurried from the throne room.

'I swear everything I have told you is true,' said the Doctor. 'I learned about the poison and its purpose from Bigon. You know that he does not lie.' The Doctor held out the hand with the micro-chips. 'Put these back! Bigon must have them back.'

Lin Futu looked at him in horror. 'You know I cannot do this.'

'You must! Listen to me, Lin Futu. I know you are a very old and a very wise man. You have been promised leadership of your people on Earth, have you not?'

'That is so.'

'Do you think for one moment that Monarch will honour that promise? Monarch wants earth for the Urbankans. The Chinese are the most populous, potentially the most powerful race on Earth. Once Monarch grasps that, what future is there for you or for your people?'

For a long while Lin Futu hesitated. Then he put out his hand and took the micro-chips. 'How can I recircuit Bigon without being discovered by Monarch. How can we get him back here unseen?'

The Doctor heaved a sigh of relief. 'Leave that to me. Is your dragon dance to be included in the recreational?'

'That is the custom.'

'Then let's make it the next item on the programme.'

'I will see that it is done.' Lin Futu bowed, and hurried out.

The Doctor moved over to Adric, whose arm was aching agonisingly by now, but he had not moved.

Carefully the Doctor took the eyepiece from him and waved him away. Adric hurried out, rubbing his arm. Seconds later, the Doctor dashed after him. Automatically the monopticon swung round, resuming its scan of the room. But there was nothing unusual to be seen.

The Doctor and Adric reached the recreational hall just as the dragon dance was beginning. They found themselves seats downstairs this time, close to the edge of the performing area, and very close to Bigon, who still sat staring blankly into space. Above their heads, the monopticon was methodically scanning the room. As it passed close to them, the Doctor gave it a wave and a smile.

In the throne room, Monarch looked at the Doctor's smiling face and sighed contentedly. 'Ah, conformity! It is the only freedom. At last the Doctor has realised that!'

The great dragon weaved its ritual dance to and fro across the room, filling the bare metal hall with swirls of colour. Winding once more around the hall, it swept close to the chairs of Bigon, Adric and the Doctor. The dragon swirled away—leaving behind it three empty chairs.

The dragon danced its way along the linkway, heading back towards the Mobilliary. It passed several monopticons along the way—but not one of them registered that the dragon had grown three extra pairs of legs during its dance.

The dragon danced into the Mobilliary, looking stangely out of place in the technological setting. The Doctor, Adric and Bicon emerged from beneath it, followed by two oriental androids, who stood waiting impassively for further orders.

The Doctor handed Adric the eyepiece and Adric dashed across the room to immobilise the monopticon.

The Doctor went over to Nyssa and started to revive her.

Lin Futu and one of his assisters led Bigon over to the operating table.

A few minutes later Nyssa was sitting up, blinking, while Bigon, his personality restored, was shaking hands with Lin Futu. 'Thank you, old friend. I am glad that you are with us now.'

At a command from Lin Futu, one of the robed assisters took Adric's place, holding the eyepiece before the monopticon. Androids don't get tired.

'What about the Princess and Kurkutji?' asked the Doctor.

'Perhaps, like Lin Futu they will join us when they hear the truth. I will summon them.' Bigon crossed to a communications console.

'What are we going to do now, Doctor?' asked Adric.

'Somehow I've got to get to the TARDIS.'

'How? It's floating out there in space.'

'It isn't all that far away. There are hatches. I must

try to reach it on a lifeline.'

Bigon returned in time to overhear him. 'Hatch nine is nearest, Doctor.'

Lin Futu signalled one of his androids. 'You will need life-support and protective covering.'

Adric found a space-pack, left in the Mobilliary since his capture. 'We've got this!'

'That won't do in the temperature out there, not for you anyway—and I'll need help.'

The android returned carrying a space-suit. 'We use this for external repairs and maintenance outside the ship,' said Lin Futu. 'In such cold, our lubrication freezes and our joints seize up!'

'Splendid,' said the Doctor. 'Adric.' Assisted by Nyssa, Adric began climbing into the suit, while the Doctor picked up the space-pack. 'And I can use this. We'll only have six minutes, though. That's as long as even I can resist sub-zero temperature.'

Soon Adric was safely fastened into the suit. Its accompanying equipment included a belt-pouch full of tools, and a long coil of polyester cord.

Princess Villagra and Kurkutji entered. Lin Futu went over to greet them—and to try and win them over to the Doctor's cause.

While they were talking, the Doctor turned to Bigon. 'Do you have control of all the simpler androids?'

'Yes. But Monarch and his ministers can countermand any order I give them.'

'Isn't there any way we could stop them?'

'Only by decircuiting them.'

The Doctor shook his head. 'There's no time for that.

Anyway, you'd be seen . . . if we could jam their link . . .'

'Wait,' said Bigon suddenly. 'Perhaps there is a way. The central control circuit has a built-in fail-safe mechanism.'

'Go on.'

'Once, faulty circuitry in the androids led to the development of independent reason, and therefore the potential for revolt. So now any collective android activity effectively jams the control circuits. Mass mutiny is impossible.'

'I see. So if we could arrange a suitable collective activity . . .'

Bigon moved to the communications console. 'I fail to see, Doctor, why one thing should not lead to another!'

Idly, Monarch surveyed the scene in the recreation hall. 'The Doctor and the boy Adric are conspicuous by their absence, to say nothing of Bigon.'

All at once, some very strange things happened. Two Greek warriors were fighting their ritual duel in the centre of the performance area—but near by two wrestlers were performing at the same time. Suddenly the troupe of Mayan dancers ran into the hall, and equally suddenly the Aborigine war dancers joined them. The central area was already packed when the Chinese dragon pranced into the hall and began weaving in and out of the other performers. The swordsmen duelled, the wrestlers struggled, the Mayans and the Aborigines *and* the dragon danced—

all together! It was a scene of utter chaos, a seething, noisy riot.

'*What is going on?*' screamed Monarch. 'Control, let it cease at once!'

The computer voice said, 'Cessation not possible. Android circuits jammed on common activity.'

Monarch was shaking with rage. 'What was designed as a fail-safe has been turned against me. The Doctor is behind this. Persuasion! Kill the girl Nyssa immediately. Find the Doctor and destroy him!'

12

Spacewalk

The Doctor and Adric were in a short corridor next to the hull, sealed by airlock doors at the end. A hatch in the centre lay open to the blackness of space.

Adric was hypnotising a hovering monopticon with the Doctor's eyepiece, while the Doctor himself was perched at the edge of the open hatchway, fastening his safety-line to a support strut. Adric wore the protective space-suit, but the Doctor had only his space-pack helmet. The corridor was airless, and very cold.

The Doctor tested the knot, climbed on to the edge of the hatchway, bent his knees, and sprang out into the blackness of space.

There, just ahead of him was the TARDIS.

With the safety-line snaking out behind him, the Doctor floated slowly towards it. He drifted closer, closer and then stopped. The TARDIS was just out of his reach.

Since he had no way to propel himself forwards, it might as well have been a hundred miles away. There was only one thing to do—the Doctor started hauling on his safety-line, pulling himself back towards the ship, in order to start again from the beginning.

His attention divided between holding the eyepiece up to the monopticon and at the same time watching the Doctor from through the hatchway, Adric failed to notice when Persuasion appeared in the airlock behind him, and then came through into the corridor, ray-gun in hand.

At the last moment, Adric sensed Persuasion's approach. He whirled round, snatched a heavy wrench from his belt-pouch and hurled it at Persuasion with all his strength.

Persuasion, like all the androids, was extremely strong, but he was also extremely light. The whizzing chunk of metal struck his chest and knocked him off his feet. He dropped the gun and Adric snatched it up.

The monopticon, freed from the hypnotic effect of the eyepiece resumed its scan, relaying the whole scene to an astonished and outraged Monarch.

'The boy has betrayed me!' he roared.

Adric levelled the ray-gun at Persuasion, who was advancing towards him, and fired—without effect, since androids are hard to kill. Persuasion leapt on him, and they were grappling furiously.

The Doctor meanwhile was pulling himself back to the ship, aware of the struggle and desperate to come to Adric's aid.

He reached the ship at last, climbed through the hatch, and flung himself into the struggle.

Seeing that the odds were not against his minister, Monarch turned to Enlightenment. 'Help him. Help him!'

Enlightenment ran from the control room.

For a while it seemed that Persuasion would be too strong for the Doctor and Adric combined. Then, with a desperate effort the Doctor ripped open Persuasion's chest cavity, extracted the vital micro-chips, and smashed them against the metal of the bulkhead. Persuasion collapsed in a heap of metal and plastic.

Monarch in the throne room gave a great cry of rage and pain.

Giving Adric a thumbs-up sign, the Doctor climbed back onto the edge of the hatch, crouched poised, for a moment, and then gave another, even more energetic, leap.

He shot out into space, quickly at first, then slower and slower as his ebbing momentum carried him closer and closer to the TARDIS. But not close enough. Not quite.

Groaning inwardly, the Doctor began pulling himself back for a third attempt.

Holding the monopticon at bay with the eyepiece in one hand, Adric stretched out and grabbed the line with the other, helping to pull the Doctor back to the ship. Once again his attention was divided—and this time it was Enlightenment who came stealthily through the airlock door. She moved silently up behind Adric, and struck him down with a single, savage blow.

Adric slumped to the floor, letting go of the rope. It was still fastened to the strut of course ... but not for long. Enlightenment moved over to the hatchway, and began unfastening the rope. The Doctor saw what was happening, but there was nothing whatever he could do about it.

The end of the rope came free, and Enlightenment cast it from the hatch. Rope and Doctor began drifting away into space. 'Farewell, Doctor,' said Enlightenment sweetly.

Watching the monitor that was functioning once again, Monarch gave a great bellow of laughter. 'Farewell, indeed. Let him drift in space, forever going nowhere!'

Still half-dazed, Adric struggled to his feet. He saw the unfastened rope, the helplessly drifting Doctor, and the smiling Enlightenment. With a yell of rage Adric threw himself upon Enlightenment, forcing her to the ground.

They fought furiously, and for a moment surprise gave Adric the advantage. But Enlightenment had fallen close to Persuasion's ray-gun. She picked it up, swung round on Adric, and fired.

Adric twisted aside just in time, and the energy-blast shattered the hovering monopticon—

—depriving Monarch of his view of events at the hatchway.

'Report, Enlightenment. Report!' he screamed.

Enlightenment was beyond reporting. Anger at his narrow escape from death, and grief at the Doctor's fate, had given Adric a sudden urge of strength. Ripping back the android skin-covering, he wrenched out Enlightenment's control circuits. Sobbing with rage, he hurled them out into space.

Breathing heavily as a result of his exertions, Adric looked down at the inert heap of metal and plastic at his feet. There was no point in being angry with it. After all, it was only a machine. He turned his mind to finding some way to help the Doctor.

Helplessly he watched the drifting figure. There seemed nothing, nothing, he could do. And time was running out.

Sadly, Lin Futu, Kirkutji, Princess Villagra and Bigon watched the Doctor from the porthole of the Mobilliary.

'Can we not get a line to him?' urged Lin Futu.

'Too late,' said Bigon sadly. 'His six minutes are almost up.'

Hovering in the blackness of space, bones and mind chilled with its icy cold, the Doctor had thought of a way to help himself. It was a ridiculously small chance, but it was all he had. With numbed fingers, he unfastened the other end of the now useless safety-line and cast it from him, watching it shake away into space.

Carefully, he took the cricket ball from his pocket, fumbling and almost dropping it. Drawing back his arm he hurled the ball at the ship with all his strength.

Unimpeded by air-resistance the ball flashed through the void, struck the side of the space ship, rebounded— and the Doctor caught it on the rebound, a perfect catch.

Its momentum carried him gently up to the TARDIS. Watched by a delighted audience, Adric from the hatchway, Bigon and the others at the port-hole, the Doctor caught hold of the TARDIS door, fished out his key, opened the door and climbed carefully inside.

Monarch, a less than delighted audience, was watching the same scene on his throne room monitors. 'I am not without agility, Doctor.' And rising with some effort, Monarch descended the steps of his throne.

Trapped inside the TARDIS, Tegan had undergone almost every conceivable emotion. She had tried keeping calm, reversing the sequence of actions that had got her in this fix. Nothing happened.

She had flung herself at the TARDIS console, hitting every switch in sight. Still nothing.

She had forced herself to be calm and study the instruction manual, only to find that she couldn't understand a word of it.

She had erupted into hysterical rage, snatching off her shoes throwing them to the ground and jumping up and down on them. Apart from hurting her feet, that hadn't achieved anything either.

Finally Tegan had slumped to the floor in a kind of despairing coma.

There was plenty of food and water in the TARDIS, unlimited room ... She would stay here, all alone until she grew old and died—unless some of those nasties from the ship managed to get at her. When the door started to open, Tegan leapt to her feet, fearing the worst.

When the Doctor came in she rushed joyously up to him. 'Doctor, how on earth ...'

Thrusting his space-pack at her, the Doctor hurried to the console, brushing her aside.

'Do be quiet, Tegan,' he said unchivalrously. 'You're spoiling my concentration!'

The Doctor studied the console, making delicately minute adjustments—easier to travel to another planet, another time than to cross those few metres of space to Monarch's ship. 'Come on old girl,' he breathed. 'Come on! Don't let me down now!'

The time rotor began to move.

The most spectacular recreational in the history of Monarch's voyages was still continuing unabated.

The fighters fought, the dancers danced, and the dragon weaved its way in and out of the crowd.

Angrily Monarch thrust his way through the gyrating throng—and stopped in astonishment when he heard a strange sound.

The TARDIS was materialising before his eyes.

As the time rotor came to a halt the Doctor snapped, 'Tegan, bring that space-pack. Come to think of it, bring another.'

Obediently Tegan went and fetched another pack. 'What are we doing, Doctor?'

'Rescuing Adric and Nyssa. Do exactly what I tell you, and do it quickly.'

'Right,' said Tegan with unexpected meekness.

When the Doctor took charge, she thought, he really took charge.

The Doctor and Tegan emerged from the TARDIS and saw Monarch glaring at them from the far side of the room. 'You sentimental fool, Doctor,' shouted Monarch above the din. He raised his voice again. 'Control! Cut all life-support atmosphere.' Monarch disappeared into the crowd.

'Quick, this way,' shouted the Doctor, and dragged Tegan away.

The Doctor and Tegan rushed into the Mobilliary to find Adric and Nyssa, surrounded by Bigon, Kurkutji, Lin Futu and the Mayan Princess Villagra.

'We are concerned for your friends,' said Bigon. 'Monarch has cut the life-support systems. We do not need to breathe, but they ...'

Adric was still wearing his space-suit, though without the helmet on as yet.

They had brought two helmets, and Adric had his own. Three helmets, four people, thought the Doctor. 'Lin Futu, have you a spare helmet?'

'One, but it is in pieces.'

'Assemble it please, as quickly as you can.'

Lin Futu hurried off, and the Doctor handed Nyssa the spare space-pack and gave Tegan his own. 'Get them on, you two. Adric, get that helmet back on!'

As the three companions obeyed, Tegan asked. 'What about you, Doctor?'

Already the Doctor was having difficulty with his breathing. 'I can go into a trance ... reduce the need for oxygen.'

The Doctor sank to the floor, sitting there cross-legged, breathing shallowly. The others waited.

'Adric!' called Nyssa.

'What is it?'

'My oxygen's running out.'

'Don't talk,' whispered Adric. 'Be still.'

The Doctor's breathing became shallower, more irregular.

Lin Futu hurried in with a helmet of a design similar to those used by the Doctor. The airline had become detached and Lin Futu began reassembling it.

Monarch felt secure when he was back on his throne. He sealed the doors and ordered the life-support system to be restored—just in the throne room. 'All I have to do now is wait—and that is something I do very well indeed.'

Working swiftly, Adric and Lin Futu completed the repairs to the helmet and slipped it over the Doctor's head.

The flow of oxygen revived him with remarkable speed and he leapt to his feet. 'Thank you, you two! Bigon, can you change the course of this ship?'

'Where to, Doctor?'

'Back to Urbanka?'

Bigon smiled and nodded.

'Good. As soon as it's done, meet me in the reception hall.'

Bigon hurried away.

The Doctor went over to the mounted poison flask and lifted it carefully from the wall. 'Monarch's poison, Adric, the only danger left on this ship. Be very careful with it.'

'What do we want it for?'

'We can't just leave it about. Anyway, I want to analyse it.'

125

'Right,' said Adric. Gingerly he took the flask.

The Doctor winked at the hovering monopticon. 'I'd go home if I were you, you won't stand an earthly where we're going!'

Monarch greeted the simple jest with a snarl of rage. 'Confound you, Doctor!' He rose. 'Control, restore all life-support.' Taking a ray-gun from a hidden locker, he descended the steps of the throne.

The Doctor turned to Lin Futu, Kirkutji and Princess Villagra. 'Come on, let's go to the TARDIS. As soon as Bigon arrives, I'm taking you back to Earth. The Urbankans can just go back where they came from!'

The Doctor led them all from the room, Adric carrying the flask.

The monster recreational was still going on when they arrived back in the hall. Perhaps it would go on forever, thought the Doctor. Perhaps the androids would dance and fight all the way back to Urbanka. It would help to keep poor old Monarch amused ...

Then, as they forced their way through the crowd to the TARDIS, Monarch appeared, barring their way, a ray-gun in his hand. 'No, Doctor,' he snarled. He levelled the weapon at the Doctor's head.

Instinctively Adric hurled the poison flask. It spun through the air and shattered at Monarch's feet, several drops splashing over him.

'Back everybody, back!' yelled the Doctor, pulling Tegan and Nyssa clear.

They stood back and saw Monarch dwindling before

their eyes. Smaller and smaller he grew, until finally he was a green blob no bigger than the frogs in the Flora Chamber pond.

The Doctor slipped off his helmet and popped it over the shrunken remains.

'Doctor, be careful!' warned Bigon, who had arrived in time to see Monarch's end.

'It's quite safe. You can take your helmets off the rest of you.' The Doctor looked down at the helmet. 'He needed an atmosphere as much as we do. Hence the Flora Chamber. Didn't you notice how there was always air in the throne room? He hardly ever left it!'

Bigon said wonderingly, 'Monarch was still in the Flesh Time?'

'Oh yes. He must have discovered some way of artificially prolonging his life, without giving up his body. The poison only works on organic matter.'

'Of course,' murmured Bigon.

'I suspected as much from the beginning,' said the Doctor modestly. 'Look at his character, all that arrogance and conceit, *very* Flesh Time! Nothing like you lot, or even his own ministers. I always had my doubts about him. I mean, someone who wants to go back in time by travelling faster than light—a fallacy of the Flesh Time if ever I heard one.'

'Can we go now, Doctor?' asked Tegan.

'Of course.' The Doctor looked at Bigon and his companions. 'Are you coming? I could take you back to Earth—that's where Tegan's going. But perhaps Monarch's death changes things?'

Bigon looked at the others, and then shook his head. 'We would have no place on Earth now, Doctor. We

127

must travel on, look for another planet, where life such as ours can go on. I will alter the course again.'

The Doctor shook hands with Bigon. 'Goodbye then, Bigon, and good luck! Come on, the rest of you, let's go.'

He ushered his companions into the TARDIS.

As he busied himself at the TARDIS console the Doctor said, 'I suppose Bigon was right. It would have been a bit tricky, settling him and the others on Earth.

'I don't know,' said Tegan cheerfully. 'They wouldn't have been a bit out of place in Terminal Three. Are we going to make it, this time, Doctor?'

'Of course. Heathrow here we come!'

Tegan sniffed. 'I've heard that before.' But she wasn't really too worried. Somehow being back in the TARDIS was rather like being home.

Tegan, Adric and Nyssa watched as the Doctor threw the main power switch and the time rotor began its steady rise and fall.

They were on their way.